MADALINE CLIFTON

Untamed

Contents

Dedications + Acknowledgements

"Untamed" is a novelette **DEDICATED** to those who are hardworking, never giving up on their dreams. It can be difficult to keep on moving yet we must keep the faith that it can be done. The burnout becomes a very real, hostile thing. "Untamed" is for the writers & authors who self-publish—a lot of hard work, am I right? "Untamed" is also for those in search of who they are on there way to who they're becoming.

It's for the people having a tough time—for the young and new adults. I wrote this short story sometime in 2020 or 2021… maybe even before then. Nobody's perfect neither is the life we were given. Just don't stop believing even when you feel like giving up. We got this!

I want to acknowledge my family—they support my 'writer dreams' which is all this seems to be. I love my brother and sister. This is definitely a novelette worth dedicating to siblings especially with the premise. The editing process was fun, enlightening and utterly mind numbing. Thank you to those of you who stuck around while also continuing to do so.

Catch Fire

Isaiah "Izzy" Sprouse was an eighteen year old boy. His eyes were a cerulean blue with short, dark brown, messy curls atop of his head. He held a sun-kissed complexion with tiny, light brown freckles splashed across his facial features. He was around five foot ten inches in height with a svelte frame. He was what most would consider lean and lanky, but he could fight if the need arose.

He was torn between the color yellow and red. He was someone who kept to himself. He was laying on his stomach when in— waltzed his older brother. He had this scowl spring to life on his face. He didn't really communicate well with others.

"What are you doing, freak?" Oliver Sprouse snarled, having once been nice towards his baby brother. He was an nineteen year old who looked an awful lot like Izzy except his eyes were a more of a sky blue. His hair held a bit of a lighter tint to it along with the older boy being taller, and a lot more reckless.

Izzy didn't respond, having returned to coloring. It helped

the boy keep his thoughts gathered, and focused. He felt his bed dip, knowing his older brother was about to push his luck.

Oliver chuckled, grabbing a fistful of his brother's hair. He saw Izzy tense before releasing a silent yelp. He smirked at how much pain he could cause the younger male who wouldn't tell a soul, "Aw, what's wrong? Can, Izzykins, no longer speak?"

Izzy shot his brother an icy glare. He was on the brink of biting Oliver who let go of his release on Izzy. "What do you want, Oliver?"

"What do you think? I have eyes and ears everywhere. Alice told me." Oliver said, growing infuriated with the younger boy.

Izzy frowned, unsure of what Oliver meant. He slowly closed his coloring book, turning over to sit on the edge of his neatly made twin sized bed. He shook his head at what Oliver was on about, "I don't know what you mean."

Oliver ground his teeth together. He moved closer to Izzy, gripping the boy as hard as possible. "My girlfriend!"

Realization lit up Izzy's cerulean blue eyes as a tint of rose pink coated his cheeks. He had been curious about what it was like to kiss someone. He had even taken his brother's girlfriend off guard when he impulsively kissed her. He wanted to know why everyone was so fascinated by the concept. He was still trying to figure it out, "I'm sorry."

"Nobody likes you, freak! I'm going to make you pay!" Oliver said, removing his grip from Izzy's shoulders. He pulled the boy to his feet, punching him in the abdomen.

Izzy grunted, feeling the agonizing pain Oliver caused him. He wanted to tell his brother to fuck off, but found it hard to breathe. "O-O—"

Oliver used his knee to cause Izzy to fall to his knees. He went in for another punch, causing blood to gush from the nose of his brother. He was enjoying the adrenaline rush that causing Izzy pain brought him. "I cannot believe my luck."

"Stop it!" Izzy yelped with a bit of an accent, laced into his tone. His brother snatched the boy up by the dark hoodie over his red long sleeve. He disliked what Oliver did to him, "Let me go!"

"Izzy, I don't think you understand how stupid the action of your consequence is. I am going to beat the stupid from you!" Oliver noted, beginning to undo his belt to whip the boy.

Izzy had tears, streaming down his cheeks. He wasn't about to let Oliver scar him further. In his bitter anger towards Oliver, he didn't think twice about what would happen. He placed his hands to Oliver's chest to shove the older boy away from him.

A sizzling sensation began to emanate from the touch of Izzy, causing a sharp pain to take hold of Oliver.

"Leave me be!" Izzy shouted as blue flames began to burn bright from his palms, burning the likes of Oliver. He didn't mean to cause Oliver to catch fire, but that's exactly what happened.

Oliver growled, releasing his grip on Izzy. He was engulfed entirely by blue flames causing the air to be filled with ear splitting screams.

Izzy's heart was beating wildly in his chest. He glanced down at his palms engulfed in blue flames. He was tempted to run away, but knew his parents would find him. He didn't want to be abandoned by those he was raised by, but he could sense with the burned body of Oliver that it would happen. He would never forgive himself for accidentally killing his older brother.

The worst of the night hadn't even come for the slightly autistic eighteen year old boy. He was horrified by himself.

Orphaned

"What did you do to your brother?" The mother of Izzy roared as tears, streamed down her pale cheeks.

His father didn't look quite so happy either.

Izzy didn't run like he yearned to do. He knew his parents would think of him as a monster. His fingers were wound into his curls as a look of panic clung to his tanned features. "I'm sorry."

"Why would you hurt, Oso? He never did anything wrong to you!" Izzy's mother screeched, wanting to slap the boy across the face. She refrained from lashing out at her only son.

"He never did anything wrong, because you always held him on a high pedestal. He bullied me." Izzy said, giving a slight shake of his head. He had come to a stop in his tracks from pacing.

"Boy, don't you take that tone with me!" Izzy's mother growled at him.

His father was wondering what he should do about the boy's murderous ways. He stood up from his armchair, stroking the

5

beard on his chin. "I think we should take him to the orphanage."

Izzy's worst nightmare was coming to fruition. He vigorously shook his head at his parents, "You can't!"

His mother held up the back of her hand. She gave him one good whack to the side of the face.

Izzy groaned as his face stung from where the woman laid her hand on him. He lightly coughed, causing blood to gurgle from the side of his mouth. How was all of this happening to him at such a young age? He feared he might have been cursed for doing something, he shouldn't be doing. He took a step back from his birth mother.

"You don't tell your father what he can and can't do. He brings home the bacon." Izzy's mother snarled at him, before glancing at her husband who was in a war with himself.

Izzy hadn't been close with his parents like he wanted to be. He would try to associate with them, but they were always busy. When he wanted to talk about his day, Oliver beat him to being the center of attention. He would always become so frustrated by being put on the back burner. Why had he been born if he was going to be ignored a good chunk of his life?

Ironically enough, his clothes weren't even his own. They were hand me downs from his brother. His parents always refused to buy him anything new including where school was concerned. He was eventually taken out of public school so his parents could get away with more neglect on his part. "I'm sorry, but, please, don't send me to the orphanage?!"

His father eyed him like he had grown a second head. "You burned our only good son alive. Why would we keep a serial killer in the making?"

Izzy felt his bottom lip tremble. He always did what they told him, no matter how absurd it sounded. He didn't ever question them, but Oliver always loved to challenge his parents. His eyes refreshed with new tears, "I d-didn't mean to!"

"I'm sure no serial killer meant to kill, but we can't take that chance." His father shook his head, shooting his wife a sour glance.

The mother placed a hand on her abdomen. "Especially, not with the new baby on the way."

Izzy's cerulean blue eyes widened at the mention. How could his mother avoid telling him about the new child? Then again, when did the woman who birthed him yet didn't love him tell him anything? He did love his mother always treating her with respect, but he never cared for the physical or verbal abuse she would dish out to him. "How can I have fire magic if one of you knew absolutely nothing about it?"

His father sighed, taking off his glasses to polish them. He replaced them on his face before answering the curly haired boy, "Fire magic is a curse, placed onto the born babe by the family who betrayed someone of another family."

He didn't understand why they treated him like a child when he acted more adult than they did. He knew how to care for himself. He was simply tired of everything including existing. "How is it a curse?"

His father didn't really want to tell him anything. He wanted to be done with the dangerous boy. "Izzy, I told you as much as I can. Go pack a bag!"

Izzy felt his bottom lip quiver, "I'm your baby boy. How can you just get rid of me?"

"You killed Oliver for no reason!" His mother screeched, needing to calm down before she lost the baby girl inside of her.

Izzy took a few deep breaths. He was tougher than they were.

He would have to leave in the middle of the night. He couldn't be dumped off at an orphanage where people his age were treated worse off.

Buttercup

He stumbled around, during the cold of the night. He was beginning to freeze to death. He had on the clothes he left home with. As soon as he saw the burned, charred body of Oliver Sprouse he knew he couldn't stay. He packed a change or two of clothing in a black backpack before taking off.

Izzy didn't know where he would go, but he knew he had to keep from being placed in an orphanage. He shivered due to how cold, and damp it had been outside. His eyes trailed up to the stars, twinkling in the night sky shining as bright as ever. He was amazed by how tiny they were. He had been walking at a fast pace from sundown to present.

His legs were growing sore. He had sharp pain radiating from his toes upwards. How could walking cause one person so much pain? He wondered how long he had been walking for him to be so achy, and exhausted. He was half tempted to climb into a dumpster in the back of a store.

Who would look for a murderer such as himself? Would anybody care about somebody like him? His parents wouldn't care since they have proved over and over; for years they didn't. His heart dropped in his chest. He'd only known one person to ever show him an ounce of kindness nor could he figure out why she would.

He sighed, beginning to yawn. He stretched an arm into the sky, throwing a curious glance over his shoulder. He didn't want to run into any trouble as he mindlessly hoisted himself onto the side of a dumpster. He needed to get a bit of shuteye if he were going to continue forth with his venture of finding somewhere he belonged. He had never felt more empty then when everything that happened— had to happen.

Izzy chose to sit in the corner of the dumpster, attempting to get as comfortable as one could in his situation. He brought his legs up to his chest, encircling his long arms around them to keep himself warm. The temperature was freezing out, during the time of night he had willingly left home. He had dried blood on his face nor could he be bothered with wiping it away. He still didn't know who he was.

He was like any other eighteen year old, except he did know what he wanted in life unlike the wish washy brats who wronged him. He wanted to be loved like the movies he would catch on the TV where people his age did have loving families. He never had that, but he always envied those who did. His eyes began to droop shut while trying to find some place of warmth, comfort, and feeling of being safe. His frantically beating heart began to slow down to a normal rate so he could doze off.

Izzy slept soundly. Everything in his head, seemed normal as he slept. He didn't awake until the noise of low whispering voices interrupted his thoughts. He pried open an eye to drink in his surroundings. He grew alarmed as soon as he found; he was no longer in the dumpster.

He was in a place that appeared to be a cathedral. He tried to find his voice as he sat up. He found he was on a tiny mattress in the midst of other beds, scattered about the place. He wasn't in an orphanage, was he? A new panic erupted in his chest, but he could cry no more.

Izzy told himself it would be best if he grew cold towards outsiders. If he was nice to everybody they would take it for weakness.

"What's your name?" A delicate, female voice asked, belonging to a woman, holding a clipboard hovered about close by. Her gentle, brown eyes remarked Izzy with such kindness it hurt.

Izzy couldn't speak. He searched his mind, but no words were formidable from his mouth. He was like a fish out of water. He might as well as not have had a name, considering the curse he bore. The life he left behind as Izzy Sprouse no longer existed, so, why continue using the name of someone he didn't know?

All he wanted to know is how he ended up in an orphanage. His eyes lazily gave the filthy place a double take. He knew those present would be trouble even if the caretakers were kind. "I don't have a name."

The caretaker sighed, "I'm Clancy Adams. I run this place. How can you not have a name?"

Izzy had grown bitter in his short time at the orphanage. He shrugged, "I just don't. How did I end up here?"

Clancy Adams wrote something on her clipboard. She was taking notes. "Alright, well, we'll have to name you. As for the other, the garbage guys found you in the dumpster, and assumed you were one of ours. Unfortunately, I would remember you as I have the other boys."

Izzy grimaced. He said nothing as something clicked in the

brown eyes of the woman.

"Buttercup suits you." Clancy said which is how Izzy got stuck with his new name.

The Beat Down

Giovanni Kitsch was a nineteen year old boy who kept to himself. He pressed his back into the cool, concrete of the building as he lit a cigarette. He was a slender, lean, lanky boy who drove the girls at his school insane. Too bad, his parents decided to forget he existed when his mother birthed him. He wasn't overly popular, but the rumor mill spread it around that he was a bad boy since he didn't associate with too many people his age.

He didn't like the way they spoke about women. He wore dark clothing with his dark pants usually having been ripped. He didn't tell anyone at school that he was from St. Orlando's Orphanage for all boys. Why would he? If he told them then they would surely go after him like they could touch him.

Giovanni stood at five foot nine inches in height with an olive complexion. He had short, jet black messy curls with silvery gray eyes that stood out to most. He couldn't be bothered with most people as he exhaled sharply. He took a few drags of the cigarette he lit. He had never felt calmer until his eyes landed on the likes of the new boy.

He had no bonds with the other boys in the orphanage nor did he try. He vaguely recalled the past life with the family who gave him up that he didn't have. He would think about his family late at night, wishing he could see how they lived. In his dreams, he swore he saw them only for the mother to freak out in German, jabbing a finger in his direction. He could hardly make out what the hissing woman would say which saw him furrow his eyebrows in confusion at her.

It was like a tug for Giovanni. If he didn't know any better then he would assume it was astral projection. His anger was what would drive him away from a life he could never have. He shook his head, finishing his cigarette before searching for the new boy. His silvery gray eyes landed on the curly haired boy who was around his age.

He felt like the new boy was probably a smidge younger than he was. He pursed his lips, wondering if he should even bother with making the new boy feel welcome. He didn't think it would help nor was he in the mood to be friendly. He chose to continue keeping to himself as he saw the sad, new boy turn bitter, cold, and angry.

"Gio! What did Clancy say about smoking?" One of the other boys, called to the dark haired boy.

Giovanni shot a glare at the fellow orphan. "Leave me the fuck alone, Kai. We've been over this. You keep trying to be my parent and I'm going to kick your ass."

Kai was always trying to look out for Gio. He thought the boy was like a brother to him. He tried to be close to the fellow dark haired boy, but Giovanni always pulled away from him.

In all honesty, Giovanni found Kai creepy nor did he like the way the year older boy attempted to hang all over him. He was on the brink of burning the caramel complected boy with one of his cigarettes. He had his reasoning for not liking Kai.

"Gio!" Kai called, moving to stand in front of the boy with dark curls. He didn't see why the younger boy kept rejecting him. He thought they were friends while hoping to be more.

Giovanni had caught Kai messing with one of the other, younger boys one evening. He didn't think anyone would be back from the afterschool programs, so since he wanted to get in a good cigarette smoking session; he stepped out. He had come across Kai taking advantage of a boy he shouldn't have been messing with. "Kai, I'm warning you!"

Kai lifted his palms, placing them on Giovanni's chest. He was trying real hard to fuck with the younger boy. He was one of the more messed up orphans who wasn't into the same gender— his parents had screwed him up so badly. He just liked causing those he saw weaker pain. "Gio, no one has to know."

Giovanni knew what Kai was trying to do. He knew why the older boy did what he did. He wasn't about to let someone mess with him, considering he had never shown interest in the same sex. "I warned you."

Kai bawled up his fists, taking aim at Giovanni's abdomen before the younger boy could stop him. "You might have warned me, but I'm not as stupid as you, little bitch!"

Giovanni grunted about to block another hit from Kai who swept his feet from underneath him. His palms became scraped from breaking his fall as did his poor knees. He got the beat down of a lifetime from Kai even when he felt he deserved it.

Bubbles

"Are you alright?" A thicker voice asked, towering over Giovanni. The boy crouched down, helping to block the sun from the silver gray orbs of Giovanni.

"Who are you?" Giovanni grunted, pushing himself into a sitting position. He felt sick to his stomach as he noted it was the newer boy.

He smirked, "You can call me, Buttercup. It's my new name. My old one is attached to my past life where my parents didn't want me."

Giovanni frowned, gesturing for Buttercup to sit beside him. "Clancy gave you the name, didn't she? She's more of a mother then anyone I've met."

Buttercup reluctantly sat down by Giovanni, "Yes, she did."

Giovanni slowly nodded, inhaling deeply while hoping the pain in his stomach would subside. He wanted to get back at Kai, but knew what happened to the other boy wasn't his fault. "My parents didn't want me either. I never met them. I hardly even remember them."

Buttercup brought his legs to his chest. He sat with Giovanni in wonderment. "What's your name? You know mine."

Giovanni snorted, shaking his head at the other boy. "I know your new nickname. I don't know your actual name. How would that be fair?"

Buttercup grimaced, pressing his lips into a thin line. "How about giving yourself a new name? You don't have to have the one attached to your old life."

Giovanni sighed, "I would love a new name. I hate my given name. What good does a full, given name do except get you in trouble? It's never worth it."

"You have the power to change it. What suits you?" Buttercup asked, tilting his head to look at Giovanni.

Giovanni shrugged, "I'm not entirely sure. I guess, I'll have to stick with my nickname that derives from my name."

"Nonsense." Buttercup muttered, growing annoyed with the older boy. He sighed, choosing to get to his feet while waiting for Giovanni to get to his.

"Where are you going?" Giovanni worriedly inquired, feeling as if the newcomer was his responsibility. He grunted while using the support of the wall to get to his wobbly feet.

Buttercup smirked. He knew somebody who was good at giving nicknames. "We're going to see, Clancy Adams. She can help with giving you a new name."

Giovanni grew doubtful, "I've known her all my life. I don't think she would have one for me. If she does, it can't be good from what other people say about me."

Buttercup glanced over his shoulder at Giovanni. "I think you're wrong. Are you coming or not?"

Giovanni groaned, but nodded his head. He followed after the fast paced boy who was eager to talk to the head of the orphanage.

The two boys found themselves in a small, but cozy office which was more comforting than the rest of St. Orlando's Orphanage. They were sitting in brown leather armchairs in front of a desk.

Clancy Adams was a delicate, frail, old woman who was pleased to have their company. She was always trying to get people to adopt the boys whenever she could. She was currently looking into therapy for Kai. She set a cup of herbal tea in front of the two boys who came to visit her.

"What can I do for you, boys?" Clancy asked, placing her hands on top of the desk.

Giovanni's leg began to bounce due to his nerves, "I was told you could give me a new name. I don't think it's possible."

Clancy softly smiled at him, "I see Buttercup told you about my naming system. It's not something I'm on my a-game about."

"If you could, what would you call him?" Buttercup asked, jabbing a finger at Giovanni.

"For a nickname?" Clancy inquired, analyzing Giovanni from head to toe. She grew thoughtful as she mulled over what name she could give to Giovanni Kitsch if it were her decision.

"Yes, for a nickname. I don't think Buttercup understands that when a boy is adopted, they would need his actual name." Giovanni said, snickering as the blue eyed boy full on glared at him.

"I probably will never be adopted. I accidentally set my brother on fire. Who would want a murderer?" Buttercup angrily remarked, returning to the cold, bitter facade he had before he tried being open with the dark haired boy.

Giovanni frowned at the confession, "I, uh—"

"Bubbles is the perfect nickname for you, don't you think?

You almost always try to help those around you." Clancy rattled off to Giovanni, interrupting the boy who furrowed his eyebrows at the name.

"Bubbles, it is." Buttercup solemnly spoke, having not drank the herbal tea. He set it on the desk, retreating deeper into himself. He began to shut down as he got up, and scurried off to be by his lonesome.

Giovanni wanted to reach out to Buttercup to let him know; he wasn't alone. Of course, he had never murdered anyone yet he still managed to get into a fight upon occasion.

Astral Plane

Giovanni was dripping in sweat. He tossed, turned and punched out in his sleep. He was having what he assumed to be nightmares. "Just stop!"

"It's time to wake up, Bubbles!" The bitter tone of Buttercup spoke, slightly shaking the older boy.

Giovanni didn't want to wake up. He was hardly getting as much sleep as he needed. He felt like he was wandering the halls of a school he never went to. "Get off me!"

Buttercup recoils, shooting a glare of daggers at Giovanni. He didn't like being popped when he did nothing wrong. "School."

Giovanni had bore witness to how withdrawn the younger boy had become. He could tell Buttercup could care-less about the world around him which was unsettling to him. "Are you alright, Buttercup?"

"Clancy wants you to show me around the school. Get dressed!" Buttercup muttered, mostly to himself more than anything.

Giovanni grunted, removing the blanket from his body. He

rubbed his eyes, unable to believe his ears. "We're not in the same grade."

"I skipped a grade. Shut up and get dressed!" Buttercup growled, losing a bit of patience with the older boy. He was dressed in a yellow long sleeve, blue jeans, and sneakers. He was ready to get the day over with, seeming unusually grumpy already.

Giovanni didn't like to take orders from those younger than him. He knew he had to get ready for the day so he did. He loved wearing dark clothing since it was a mood for him. He didn't bother with his messy curls as he snatched up his backpack. He nor any of the boys might not have had the best looking items, but they worked for whatever was needed.

He grumbled to himself as the day dragged on. He carried his pack of cigarettes in his jacket pocket with his lighter. He would need a few before the day was over. He didn't even want to go to class. "Slow your roll, kid!"

Buttercup came to a stop at the school entrance. "I'm not a kid."

The walk to the high school was a short distance from where they lived.

"Sorry, Buttercup." Giovanni corrected himself, shooting the brunette an apologetic look. "How do you expect for them to take you seriously if you don't have a name?"

Buttercup didn't reply, "Orlando Adams High School?"

"It's in dedication to the son and husband of Clancy." Giovanni sighed, already in need of a cigarette.

Buttercup felt himself grow anxious. He didn't see what good it did to go to a red brick building full of jerks. "She told me she would meet me in the office to get my school schedule straightened out. See you later, Bubbles!"

21

Giovanni watched the younger boy stalk off. He pressed his fingertips to his temples. He was evidently annoyed by the boy who seemed to have a problem with the world. He couldn't blame Buttercup as he opted to head around to the back of the school. He leaned on the wall, pulling out his cigarette with a lighter.

He lit it, taking slow drags. He was happy when the stress in his heart began to waver. He shut his eyes for a few seconds as a pull of a tug gripped his heart. His imagination came into clear view as he saw the woman he swore he dreamed about every night. He noted the scenery was different since she was outside on her knees, sobbing like no tomorrow.

Giovanni had seen the woman a hundred times, but always found her pointing in his direction, speaking in fluent German. He still didn't know what the dreams meant— if they meant anything.

"You're in the astral plane. You can't help comfort your mother." A familiar voice startled him.

Giovanni jumped, turning while in an attempt to find the voice of Clancy Adams. He knew it was her, but how would she know what he was going through? He had been curious about the revelation of Buttercup killing his brother, but he hadn't asked the younger boy. He was scared to ask what happened where the younger boy was concerned. His eyes cut to the woman, kneeling on the ground.

So, his mother was of German origins? He guessed it made since due to his given last name. He thought he might have also been descended from Jewish culture, but he couldn't be for sure. He blinked a couple of times before pulling himself out of the so-called astral plane. He sighed, allowing his eyes to dart open only to find he was going to be late on his second day of school.

Giovanni had seen no signs of Clancy Adams even if she was supposed to meet Buttercup in the office. He swore he was losing his mind. He glared at the cigarette he finished, wondering if the damned thing wasn't making him deluded.

Blossom

Caleb Hemingway was a scrawny toothpick with fair features. His eyes were an ominous, dark brown with short, red curls atop of his head. He was about five foot ten inches in height with a lean, lanky build. He had this haunting glare in his eyes for a prep school boy who recently turned nineteen. It's not like he could leave on his own even if he wanted to.

"Caleb, what are you doing?" Nazareth Hemingway asked her son. She went by Nazz for a nickname. She was dressed in a dark blue blazer with dress pants to match. She was putting in an ear-ring as she went in search of her only son.

"I ask myself that everyday, mother." Caleb replied, shaking his head. He was dressed in his school uniform consisting of a dark blue blazer with khaki pants. He would rather be anywhere else but school with those chums of his.

"Well, Blossom, I have some news for you!" Nazz smiled, placing her hands down in front of her.

Caleb only let people close to him call him by the nickname of Blossom. It was due to his fiery head of hair along with how

24

he took charge. "Yes, mum?"

Nazz chuckled, but grew serious. "Your father and I are stopping by the orphanage this afternoon—"

Caleb perked up, interrupting his mother. "I'd like to come. Can I or would that stop them from allowing you to adopt?"

Nazz was unable to have any more children. She had miscarried after she had Caleb. It had been three years before the Doctor told her— she couldn't birth another.

Caleb had always wanted a sibling. He yearned to have people he could look out for; a sister or brother who would need him. He was overly popular at his prep school, but no one actually needed him.

"I'll talk it over with Shua. I don't think it would hurt as long as you stay in the limo." Nazz softly informed her only begotten son. She didn't want children solely for Caleb to have someone, but she wanted to be able to give someone a home who needed it. She was a petite, short woman who did a lot for other people.

She was a blonde woman with piercing green eyes.

Joshua Hemingway looked an awful lot like Caleb. He used the nickname "Shua" because it was unique. He was the first one to have called his son, Blossom. He claimed it wasn't just for the fiery hair his baby boy had, but it was also because of how red in the face his son would get when he was embarrassed.

"Do I have to go to school, today?" Caleb asked his mother who chuckled.

"Blossom, we have to set a good example for the child we will adopt. Isn't there a girl you like who makes attending worthwhile?" Nazz asked, chuckling as Caleb pouted.

"Sonya Addison," Caleb dreamily stated, shaking his head. A sad sigh escaped him as he added, "She just disappeared with no warning. She wasn't even interested in me."

"Honey, there are a lot more girls. I'm sure you'll meet someone who falls all over you." Nazz reassured, blowing the ginger boy a kiss.

Caleb sighed, "I hope you won't force my new brother to change schools. I hate prep school."

Nazz blatantly sighed. She had been meaning to talk to her son about changing to a public, less expensive school. Her husband worked as an entrepreneur while she owned a pet store.

They had the money to send their son to a wealthy school, but they wanted whatever made Caleb happy for him.

"I know, Blossom, but we can talk about changing schools after you attend. I have appointments booked until then. I love you." Nazz smiled once more at Caleb before leaving him to it.

Caleb lived in a dark oak Victorian style home, consisting of four bedrooms with three bathrooms. He knew the house was paid off since his parents wanted him to always have a stable place. To him, it was almost like a mansion since it had enough rooms, but unlike an actual mansion; it gave off a cozy, comforting, safe vibe.

There was a fireplace in the living room for when the need arose. The house sat on a good acre of fresh land, but Caleb swore it was haunted. Then again, he wondered if the Ghost Whisperer hadn't been right about people being haunted, and not places.

"Time for school." Caleb bitterly muttered, picking up his dark blue backpack. He went out to catch the bus, but found he would have to walk. He missed the bus by a minute nor was his bus driver a friendly person. His bus driver hated rich folk such as himself nor could he understand why.

He scoffed, kicking rocks as he solemnly walked in order to

get to his preppy school.

Prep School

Caleb let a tired sigh escape his pink lips. He hung his head as he roamed the halls of the prestigious, and clean prep school. He hated the prep school like no one could imagine. The only good thing about attending said school was his best friend.

"Blossom, who actually enjoys school? Prep or not?" His best friend called, appearing in the form of a blonde boy. His eyes were dark as was his complexion. He had this smile plastered across his face.

"Rory Morrison, I thought you did." Caleb smirked, allowing his best friend to steer him to their special hangout spot. His best friend was almost like a brother in his eyes.

Rory wasn't really close with anyone while trying to keep a distance. "I found out where your girl went—"

"Sonya might have been my dream girl, but she would never have been mine. Not in a million years." Caleb corrected his friend who shook his head.

Rory gripped Caleb's shoulder. "I know where she disappeared to."

"Where?" Caleb curiously asked, furrowing his eyebrows at the boy.

Rory opened his mouth to answer when the two friends were rudely interrupted.

"Rory Morrison mingling with Caleb Hemingway. This isn't what I like to see." Benjamin was the wealthiest popular kid at the prep school. He lied to get to the top along with manipulating those around him. He never could take the blame for those he continued to wrong.

Rory was shoved to the pavement of the balcony. He was helped up by Caleb who glared at the dark haired male.

"What do you want, Benji?" Caleb angrily growled at the green eyed demon.

"I made a deal with you, Powderpuff Girl. Join my ranks where life could get better for you at your time here or continue communing with filth like Rory and worsen shit for yourself. It seems as per usual you have chosen the latter." Benjamin said, uncrossing his arms as he took Rory by the collar of his blazer.

"I've told you a thousand times before that I won't join your ranks!" Caleb growled, hating how Benjamin thought he ruled everything.

Benjamin nodded, "I know." He pulled out a pocket knife, flicking it open. He thrust the blade, deep into the abdomen of Rory in hopes to watch his sacrificial lamb bleed out.

Caleb's eyes widened in horror. He was about to shove the prep school popular boy off of Rory when Benjamin shoved the boy off the balcony. "What the fuck is your problem?"

Benjamin watched in satisfaction as Caleb rushed over to peer over the balcony railing. He grew colder while darkly admitting something else disturbing to Caleb, "I needed a lamb to the slaughter for my Lord of Chaos."

Caleb tugged at his curls, having caught a glimpse of the gory scene from where Rory hit the ground. He had silent tears, streaming down his pale complexion. His anger got the best of him as he whirled around to glare at the satanic boy, "You piece of shit!"

"It's not noice to talk about yourself like that, Powderpuff." Benjamin remarked in an unfazed tone.

Caleb bawled up his fists, ready to take a swing on the rich, popular motherlover when black flames began to emanate from his palms. His eyes widened as the tears seeped harder from his dark brown eyes. "I was talking about you! I feel for the family who was cursed with you in their lives."

Benjamin shrugged, "It seems to me, you're the cursed one."

Caleb bore his teeth in a grind towards Benjamin. He took deep breaths before attempting to hit the other boy. A blast of scorching, hot, but black flames shot out of his hand towards Benjamin. He winced as Benjamin yelped as the ball of fire hit him directly. He tensed, feeling bad for something he couldn't control. "I don't think I'm cursed."

"Those with power are indeed cursed, Hemingway. Do your research!" Benjamin hissed only to disappear so Caleb couldn't get in anymore burns. He was going to have to sacrifice the redhead to his Lord of Chaos if the proper trade was to be made.

Caleb forgot all about Benjamin, eyeing his burning palms. He had long stopped sobbing with his mind briefly taken from his best friend. How could he afford to have a brother if he lost his best friend, because of how power greedy someone could be? He still didn't believe the fire magic inside was a curse, but, maybe, his way of thinking was wrong. He sighed, knowing he would have to bury someone he would never see again.

He couldn't take much more of being at his prep school.

Especially, not when people like Benjamin existed. He needed to escape even when Benjamin would continue to go on to do darker things.

Adoption

"I'm not sure I want a brother anymore." Caleb scornfully told his parents. He was sitting in the limo, outside the orphanage with them. Looking at his father was like looking in the mirror.

"You could always meet them. I know what you went through with Rory wasn't easy, but we all have to move on." Nazz gave Caleb's hand a soft squeeze.

Caleb sighed, "Fine. I won't like it." He was already put off of having a sibling like person in his life. He had lost his best friend who almost always kept him at a distance.

"Have a little faith." Shua said, exiting the limo with his wife.

Caleb refrained from exiting the limo. He had been given the okay of being allowed to speak to the other boys if he wanted. He heard the head of the orphanage was as kind as his own mother. After a few minutes of boredom, he decided to exit the limo to get a breath of fresh air. He found it odd how hardly any of the orphan boys were enjoying such a beautiful, but chilly day in the gentle warm gold rays of sun.

His eyes briefly flickered to the building. Why stay cooped

up all the time when you could so easily be outside, enjoying every aspect of nature? He walked up to the fence, unable to comprehend the ludicrous children of the latest, and by far worst generation. He did catch sight of one particular boy with dark brown curls, sitting on pavement in a crisscross applesauce manner. He squinted his dark eyes to figure out what the boy was doing since he appeared to be toying with his hands.

Caleb made out a small ball of blazing blue flames dancing in one of the palms of the curly haired boy. He recalled the dark flames he produced, stirring some relief in his heart. For a while, he thought he was going crazy since it happened to him—once. He wanted to call out to the boy to get his attention, but his eyes were on the tamed blue flames. He wondered if he could convince his parents to adopt the boy who appeared to be just like him.

The boy seemed to sense someone watching him. He used his mind to put out the flame before his deep blue eyes trailed up to meet the dark brown orbs of a stranger. He slowly rose to his feet, dusting off his palms on the bottom of his blue jeans. He walked over to the fence, scowling as he went along. He came to a stop in front of the strange ginger, keeping eye contact with him the entire way.

"What's your name?" Caleb asked the blue eyed boy.

"Buttercup." He replied, shifting uneasily on his feet. He didn't open up or become friendly with the stranger. In fact, he didn't care for the dark eyed boy.

"I'm Blossom." Caleb said, softly smiling as he stuck a hand towards Buttercup through one of the holes in the fence. He could tell the younger boy was oddly reserved, seeming to already not like him for whatever reason. He added, "I don't bite" as a precaution.

Buttercup took a step back from Blossom. A pout lit up his features as he spoke next, "I do, bite."

Caleb was taken back by what the younger boy said. He wondered what Buttercup meant when out rushed another, curly haired boy. He took note of the direction the dark haired boy was heading. "Hey, you! What's your hurry?"

Buttercup immediately scurried over to the dark haired boy, clinging to him as he whispered something to his friend.

A scowl lit up the silvery gray eyes of the dark haired boy who angrily strode over to glare directly at the ginger. "Strangers aren't welcome here!"

Caleb frowned, taken back by the cold demeanor of the orphans. He didn't know what he had been expecting. After all, the boys were orphans while he kept wondering why they were so cold. He sighed, hanging his head in defeat as he returned to the inside of the limo. He seemed to think there was something more to the two orphan boys who he briefly met.

His parents returned not too long after.

"The boy we want is around your age, Blossom, but there's an exception." Nazz softly cooed to her son.

Caleb furrowed an eyebrow, "What's the exception?"

"It's a little bit harder to explain. Just know, this means you're not getting one brother, but two." Shua said, causing excitement to spring to life in the dark eyes of his son.

"Do they have names?" Caleb eagerly inquired. He was happy about the news, but he was still partially torn on the subject after the death of Rory Morrison.

"Isaiah Sprouse and Giovanni Kitsch." Nazz replied, gently smiling.

Caleb couldn't wait to properly meet them.

Not So Sweet

"I do not want to go live with rich people!" Izzy growled, viciously at Bubbles. He still didn't care to know the name of the older boy. He had this sour scowl plastered across his tanned features.

"Buttercup, I know—" Bubbles opened his mouth to speak only to be rudely interrupted.

Izzy began to realize how childish the nickname he was gifted seemed. He sighed, dropping his shoulders. "They won't love us properly."

Bubbles rolled his silvery gray eyes to the blue skies of the day. He was trying to convince Buttercup to go pack. He had been informed of the adoption process where the younger boy would join him. He was happy, because he thought of the blue eyed boy as an annoying brother. One he never had in his life before the new boy showed up at the orphanage.

"Buttercup, how do you know—?" Bubbles was in the midst of asking when Izzy grew tired causing him to cut his question short.

Izzy released another annoyed sigh. He tugged on the end of his dark blue long sleeve shirt. His cerulean blue eyes trailed up to meet the smirk in the gray eyes of Bubbles. He shook his head at the older boy, "Can you not call me that?"

Bubbles shifted from one foot to the other. What else was he supposed to call the younger boy? He pulled out a cigarette, flickering open his lighter to take a few drags, puffing in the process. He was more stressed than he would like to admit. "What do I call you then?"

Izzy grimaced, waving the smoke of the cigarette from the entrance of his nostrils. "You can call me, Izzy."

Bubbles felt relief stir in him. At least, the younger boy was starting to trust him. "Well, Izzy, I'm Giovanni."

Izzy didn't reply. His days at Orlando Adams High School were brutal due to how difficult he was during the school hours. He had bitten the principal's hand when the guy clamped a hand down on his shoulder. He didn't apologize so he was expelled right off the bat, but Clancy Adams did what she did best. He would be returning to the school in the next week nor did he desire to do so.

"I don't even want to go to school next week." Izzy gently revealed while adding, "Can I drop out?"

"Izz, education is important. I'll be with you every step of the way." Bubbles said, feeling all tingly from the stress relief the cigarette brought him. A small smile began to surface to his lips as he gently smacked them in satisfaction.

Izzy dropped his gaze to the pavement, "What if I accidentally set the school on fire? You know with my ability?"

Bubbles chuckled, "Izz, you won't. You can control yourself."

"I set my big brother on fire by accident. He was bullying me for one measly incident." Izzy confessed in a low whisper, casting a glance about to make sure no one overheard his slipup to Giovanni.

Bubbles sighed, putting his cigarette out before turning to face the brunette boy. "Izz, we all have a past. Nothing happens on purpose. Otherwise, life would be boring."

Izzy smiled, fully aware of how right his brother was. He already cited Bubbles as an older brother except he was closer to him then his own blood brother. He was still upset over what he did to someone who didn't deserve to die the way he had. If there was one thing he could change then it would be the death of Oliver Sprouse. "I guess you have a point, Bubbles."

Bubbles frowned, "I told you my name, no? It's actually Giovanni. Gio for short."

Izzy gave a nonchalant shrug to the older boy. A smirk remained glued to his features, "So? I'll call you what I prefer."

Bubbles extended a hand to ruffle the dark brown curls atop of Izzy's head.

Izzy ducked, avoiding the contact. His action caused Giovanni to tilt his head at him, gifting him a funny— pointed look.

"Izzy, I won't bite you." Bubbles said, furrowing his eyebrows at how serious the eighteen year old had grown.

Izzy shrugged, "Like I told, the ginger boy I will bite you. I don't fancy other people touching me."

Bubbles ran his fingers through his own, jet black curls. "Sorry, Izz. I didn't mean to cross a boundary."

Izzy was seemingly happy, bubbly, and bright around certain people. His shoulders visibly relaxed, "I know. I didn't tell you. It's not your fault."

"Izz, they'll be here at noon. You should really pack." Bubbles frowned, growing strict with the boy.

"I don't really want to be adopted, Gio!" Izzy angrily rattled off. He would rather stay at the orphanage. He already held a connection with the caretaker. He enjoyed how motherly Clancy Adams was to him.

"Izz! Would you rather be adopted alone?" Bubbles curiously asked, hoping the boy would change his mind.

"They only wanted you!" Izzy accused, scowling at Bubbles. He wasn't stupid. He knew nobody could want him after what he did. He truly did believe he was cursed.

Difficulty

Izzy had tears, streaming down his fair cheeks. He had hidden himself from those at the orphanage. He didn't want to be found, considering he knew how unwanted he was. A new thought began to tug at him— what if he took off on his own again? His parents couldn't even be bothered to come find him, making him aware that they hadn't been joking about dumping him at the orphanage.

He tugged at his curls as tears began to blur his vision. He hated the cruel, unusual, cold truth. He wouldn't change the past even if he could, because then he would still be in a broken home. His heavy breathing was causing his body to shake due to his nerves. His emotions were collapsing in on themselves.

Why was he feeling so upset over something he couldn't change? Izzy was the unattached, unemotional, but happy eighteen year old who turned everything to ash with one touch. He took a few deep breaths as he regained his composure. He wiped away the stray tears, attempting to dry on his face. He narrowed his deep blue eyes, opting to scowl as if he had been burned himself.

As he sat there, collecting himself with his thoughts— Bubbles was searching all over for him.

"Izzy!" The voice of Bubbles caused the eighteen year old to jump, knocking his head on the roof of the isolated desk he hid under.

Izzy wanted to lash out for the pain, starting in his skull. He mentally yelped at the contact before gently brushing his fingertips over his temples. He needed to keep calm before he lost all sense of control. He was still slightly shaking from the events of the day, needing some personal space from everyone at the moment. He kept wishing he could be a normal eighteen year old; instead, holding no hope for his future.

"Izzy, where the fuck are you?" Bubbles angrily called into the dusty air. He was even more annoyed, considering the clock was ticking. He chose to pack for the both of them since Izzy was choosing to be stubborn.

Izzy kept to his safe space. He wouldn't be forced to go where he wasn't wanted. His eyes were tightly shut as he nearly fell asleep.

"Ah, Buttercup! There you are!" The soft voice of Clancy Adams nearly gave Izzy a heart attack. The elderly woman was peering at him— under her desk with worry laced into her homey eyes.

His eyes shot open in a panic as he shook his head at her, "I don't want to go!"

"Alas, but you have too, sweet boy. There's a time for everything." Clancy gently remarked, motioning for Izzy to come out from under the desk.

Izzy was reluctant, but did as she suggested. He stood up, brushing off the dust from his blue jeans. His eyes set on the woman who took a seat at her desk, "What about you?"

A sadness swept into her brown eyes. "I can't continue to keep this place running by myself nowadays. No one is interested in caring for abandoned, orphaned children anymore."

Izzy felt a sting in his heart. "You can't give up!"

Clancy chuckled, shaking her head at him. "Isaiah, I'm not giving up. I can't keep it up, and not because I don't want to. I'm an old woman who can't take much more strain on my heart."

Izzy grimaced, "How about I stay to help you?"

Clancy chuckled, shaking her head at the brown haired boy. "No, you have to go live your life. I admire how you want too, but it's best we both move on."

Izzy could tell he wasn't going to win the conversation they were having. "What will happen to you?"

"Well, once I see you and Gio off then I can retire. I should have when my husband passed away, but I wanted to keep the orphanage open for as long as I could. Like I said, I'm old nor can I do much more for those in this environment." Clancy said as if she knew a secret he didn't.

"You've been so kind to me." Izzy said, sniffling a little bit. He shook off the emotions that ran deep in his veins. He wouldn't break down anymore, because it wouldn't change the outcome of his future or even the past.

Clancy sighed, "You and Gio have been adopted. I got Kai a good home with therapy sessions. I do believe he will get better. I always will, because what's worse than this?"

Izzy had a few suggestions of what could be worse. He shook it off, scratching his curls due to his nerves. He shifted about to rattle off one of his thoughts when Bubbles interrupted.

"Izzy, I've been looking everywhere for you! What the fu—fudge, have you been doing? I packed for you!" Bubbles said, gently tugging on Izzy's arm who shoved him away.

"I was speaking with the head of the orphanage." Izzy nearly spat at the older boy, keeping to his bratty, bitter attitude.

Bubbles rolled his eyes to the ceiling, hiding the annoyance of irritation Izzy caused him. Why did the younger boy act so bratty? He sort of understood why Izzy was cold, but bratty?

"You won't need what you've packed. I'm sure the Hemingway family will have clothes for you." Clancy said, causing Izzy to furrow his eyebrows.

"They'll probably have clothes only rich people would want to wear." Izzy replied, scowling as he grew awfully silent.

New Home

Izzy threw the Victorian style home a hateful glare. He wanted to return to the orphanage where he had felt safer than anywhere he had been prior. He was about to turn about face when Bubbles grabbed a hold of him to shove him forward.

Nazz had been the only one present to get them since her husband had a work emergency. "You don't have to switch schools. Caleb should be waiting to show you around the house. Be good, boys!"

"Where are you going?" Bubbles rose a curious eyebrow at the woman.

Izzy folded his arms to his chest in utter bitterness. He should have known the woman adopting them wouldn't care how they fared. He slowly, silently shook his head in glaring disapproval.

"You'll see, come, dinner time." Nazz beamed, returning to the limo.

Bubbles had to drag Izzy all the way up the pavement to the cherry red, double oak door. "Stop it, Buttercup!"

Izzy almost burned Bubbles as he shoved the older boy off of him. "Why don't you go fuck yourself off a cliff?"

Bubbles was about to make a smart remark when the doors swung open to reveal an unamused Caleb Hemingway.

Izzy remembered the ginger lad who went by Blossom. He scowled equally as hard at the insane redhead, yearning to be elsewhere.

"You two are fighting like brothers." Blossom noted, motioning for the two boys to enter the home.

Izzy pouted, keeping a distance from the *eldest of* the two. He didn't inch any closer to Giovanni, hating his own mind as they followed the redhead.

Bubbles straightened his posture. He thought about extending a hand towards the redhead to shake, thinking better of it. Instead, he cleared his throat to speak, "I'm Giovanni Kitsch, Gio, or Bubbles."

"My name is Caleb Hemingway or Blossom." Caleb smiled, extending his hand to shake with Giovanni. He was happy one of the two orphan boys was glad to meet him.

Bubbles and Izzy gawked at how beautiful, elegant, and cozy the Hemingway way home was. They hadn't seen anything more hauntingly, beautiful.

Izzy refrained from scoffing to showcase the bitter, dark thoughts still kicking around in his tiny brain. He needed to get it together yet found it to be a difficult task. He decided to keep quiet for the time being.

"This one is Isaiah Sprouse, Izzy, or Buttercup." Bubbles finally spoke for an uncaring Izzy. He almost placed a hand on the shoulder of the brunette boy until he recalled earlier. He dropped his hand down by his side, softly smiling at Caleb.

Izzy didn't want the other boy to know his name. He truly didn't like Caleb, "That's not my name!"

"Izz, you don't have to continue to be difficult. Caleb is our new brother." Bubbles said, gaining an eye roll from Izzy.

Izzy was about to make another, nasty remark when Caleb cleared his throat to kill the tension, breaking up the monotony.

"How about I show you the bedrooms? I have something I have to take care of anyway." Caleb said, seeming to be hurt by the way Izzy was behaving towards him. What did he do wrong to make the younger boy already dislike him?

"This place is unsafe. Can we not return to the orphanage?" Izzy rattled off to Bubbles, acting like Caleb didn't exist or couldn't hear him.

Caleb cleared his throat, "St. Orlando's Orphanage is being torn down to make room for a nature park or something. I don't know when, but it's what I heard through the grapevine. You're stuck with us, Isaiah."

"You heard wrong." Izzy vehemently spoke, further saddening Caleb who thought he found brothers in the pair before him. He could tell Giovanni wasn't as put off by the idea.

Caleb sighed, gesturing for them to follow him up the stairs. "I'm going to show you to your bedrooms then I'm going to attend to my business."

Bubbles shook his head at Izzy. He didn't wait for the stubborn boy as he trudged up the stairs with red velvet carpet. He would have slapped Izzy had he believed it would help.

Izzy blew a raspberry at the two. He was hesitant to follow at first, despising being somewhere new. He didn't want a new home even if it meant a brighter future. Why couldn't he be surrounded by a few good people who had his best interest at heart? He slowly trudged behind the other two boys, truly disliking how big the house was.

If one were to ask Izzy then he wouldn't skimp on telling

you how creepy it was. Sure, an insane person might think it was cozy, but in no way did he think it was cozy let alone homey. He began to think of the barely audible goodbye he said to Clancy Adams before he was taken from the orphanage. He was partially happy that he wasn't being adopted without Bubbles. He didn't know what he would do if he had to be by himself at an orphanage that was obviously going bankrupt.

He did feel guilty about behaving the way he did towards Caleb. He knew the ginger seemed alright, but he wasn't ready to form a tight knit circle with a third boy. He could tell his actions hurt Caleb, but did he care? He needed to be alone to gather his thoughts then he might feel differently towards the strange, ginger haired lad.

"What is your mother going to do? She mentioned something about us, seeing at dinner." Bubbles curiously spoke, catching the attention of Izzy.

Caleb immediately perked up. He stopped at a bedroom door, "She's making a special dinner to welcome you into the home. It's a tradition when someone new comes along."

Bubbles smiled whereas Izzy frowned. "I'd love to learn to cook. I'd like to learn to make Jewish food."

Caleb shook his head at Bubbles, "You need to speak to a professional about making Jewish food then. My mom couldn't make Jewish food to save her life."

Izzy would be glad when he could catch some shut eye. If he could sleep off his new surroundings then maybe he would be alright. A silent, sad sigh escaped his lips while Caleb finished showing them around. Exhaustion was heavy within the brunette eighteen year old boy.

Soy Bean Latte

Giovanni is staring at the small, quaint cafe with hope in his heart. He hadn't had a cappuccino in ages. He didn't think he would be able to conquer the world without a good, ole' fashioned caffeinated buzz. He gingerly brushed his fingertips across his temples with the need to wake up. He had been outright ignored by Izzy while listening to Caleb chatter away.

In short— their nicknames might have been stupid, but it was better than outsiders choosing for them, wasn't it?

He inhaled deeply to exhale slowly. He made a mention of sitting with Caleb during lunch who was new to Orlando Adams High School. He heard the ginger boy reiterate tales of what prep school was like nor did he want to know. He slowly made for the entrance of the cafe, catching a glimpse of how non-crowded it was. His eyes landed on the barista behind the counter nor did he think he would be able to speak as he drew closer.

Giovanni could feel his heart trying to claw its way from his chest. "H-hi, I'd like a soy bean latte."

The barista smiled at him. She was a nineteen year old girl who went to the same high school. She worked part time before classes. Her eyes were a light gray with long brown curls that fell all the way to her butt. She was petite in size with an hourglass figure to die for.

She was a short girl with a brown complexion. Her curls had soft pink highlights at the bottom. She was intelligent, shy, and your average nerdy girl who could be popular if she desired to be.

Giovanni had never seen someone so beautiful. He knew he knew the barista, but what exactly was her name? He was about to look for a nametag when his order was called. He didn't have time to waste, dishing out the money for his much needed caffeine.

The beautiful girl shot Giovanni a friendly smile. She seemed to want to voice something to him when her best friend waltzed in.

"Soy! Are you ready for class?" Her best friend called to her upon entering the Café.

Giovanni furrowed his eyebrows, "Soy? What kind of name is that?"

"It's a nickname." The beautiful girl sighed, taking off her apron. She rolled her eyes, extending a hand to the olive complected boy, "My name is Sonya Addison."

"Giovanni Kitsch." He said, eagerly shaking hands with her. His smile brightened at the connection they made.

The best friend calling for Sonya made her way over. Hands came to rest upon the waistline of the best friend who was also slightly pouting.

Sonya rolled her eyes, "My best friend is Fiona Calvert. Her nickname sounds close to the name of Theo, spelt F-I-O. Am I right, Fiona?"

Giovanni took in the best friend. He knew Fiona Calvert as well, rapidly blinking upon seeing her up close.

Fiona Calvert was a nineteen year old girl who took issue with the world. Her eyes were a striking emerald green with thick, brown curls that fell a little past her shoulder blades. Of course, her curls had dark blue highlights at the bottom. She was petite in her figure much like Sonya as well as being the same, short stature. She had a pale complexion with a knack for wearing dark clothing.

She was a tomboy who held such disregard for the universe. "Is this your boyfriend, Soy?"

"No, Fiona. This Giovanni." Sonya objected in a playful manner.

Fiona rolled her eyes, before releasing a stifled yawn. She drank in Giovanni, soon realizing she knew him from somewhere, but where? She shrugged, "Nice to meet you, Gio. My nickname is out then."

"Likewise and Nonsense." Giovanni found himself saying. He perked up, sipping on his soy bean latte. He mentally gagged at the taste since he wanted something favorable like a cappuccino. He lost his train of thought upon setting his sights on the likes of Sonya Addison.

Fiona jabbed a thumb in the direction of the double glass doors. "Are you two ready to become bored to death?"

"Learning is an important part of life." Sonya scolded her best friend. She was tossed her soft pink coated backpack by Fiona.

Fiona led the way out of the café, shooting Giovanni a curious look over her shoulder. "No, that's what venturing out into the world is for. You coming, stranger?"

Giovanni followed the girls from the café. He got what he

didn't really want, but found himself satisfied. He didn't know girls would want to actually hang out with him. He knew they could be as bad as guys at times. "Sonya, isn't wrong, but venturing into the world is a hard life lesson."

Sonya smirked over at Fiona. "Somebody is wise beyond his years."

Fiona grimaced, hanging her head in defeat. "I know what you mean, Gio. When you've lived a hard life then you get it. I was partly making a joke."

Giovanni placed one hand in his pants pocket. He didn't know he was going to be making new friends nor did he think it would be that easy. Of course, he had a crush on Sonya. Would he tell her? He didn't find it would be wise to ruin their newly, budding friendship.

Easy as Pie

Giovanni groaned. He wanted to opt out of class forever. He finally understood what Fiona had been ranting about that education was indeed boring. He'd rather dive into the knowledge of learning about his own Jewish heritage than the long day he was seeming to have. He had one hand, tugging at his dark curls while the other rested on the table beneath him.

"Gio!" The voice of Fiona Calvert chirped as she plopped down her lunch tray in front of him. She took a seat, using a bony finger to poke him from across the table.

Giovanni jumped as his eyes snapped open. He was so exhausted by lunchtime, he was on his way to becoming one with his meal. "Fiona!"

Fiona chuckled at his attempt to mock her. "So, there's a rumor about you spreading. I didn't believe it nor did Sonya, but…"

"Fiona, leave him alone. He looks exhausted." Sonya gently cooed from right beside him. She too was also able to startle the olive complected lad.

Giovanni became wide awake and on high alert upon hearing her speak. He felt something stir in him that he didn't know had been long dead inside of him, "Sonya?"

Sonya saw the boy beside her turn a rosy pink color. She could tell he liked her to which she liked him in return. She was sort of hoping he would find the courage to speak up, sighing when he didn't.

Fiona observed the pair, pressing her lips together in a thin line. She had caught them shooting each other glances when they had yet to talk. She was thankful they finally did speak to each other. It was getting on her nerves to see two people who liked each other; ignore each other for a good part of the semester. "Hey, back to this rumor—?!"

Giovanni blinked, returning his gaze to Fiona. "What is this rumor?"

"Well, some ginger boy mentioned you were an orphan." Sonya softly replied. She went on to add in a low whisper, "I didn't get his name, but I thought you should know."

Fiona watched Giovanni stiffen, confirming the rumor for her. She didn't care since she knew what it was like to have parents who didn't want you. Her father didn't stick around after she was born so she never met him. The mother who did raise her was verbally and physically abusive. Of course, the woman she was raised by was also a classic narcissist so the woman had to have someone to abuse.

Giovanni harshly gulped. He knew which ginger boy they were talking about. He bawled his fists up under the lunch table as his temper flared. He began to feel heat stir in his palms causing something he wasn't aware of to happen.

Sonya's eyes widened at the sight of blazing green flames emanating from his palms. She had never met someone with otherworldly powers. She heard tales of curses being placed on particular families nor did she know how true it was. All she knew is she needed to get Giovanni to calm down. She breathlessly, placed a hand on his shoulder hoping her touch was enough to soothe the dark haired boy.

Giovanni had briefly glimpsed the green flames, alarming him further. What the fuck was wrong with him? He couldn't be cursed like Izzy and Caleb, right? His breathing returned to normal from the touch of Sonya. His heartbeat returned to a slow, steady beat as his gaze saddened. "I was an orphan."

"Gio, don't sweat it. We still think you're pretty cool." Fiona said, shooing away some of the doubts Giovanni was having about being friends with anyone. She could tell the truth was eating away at the poor sap.

Giovanni felt relief stir in his heart, "Most people aren't so understanding."

"I get it, bro. You had a hard life. Who ever has it easy aside from rich people?" Fiona said, not wanting to talk about her past or her home life. She was afraid she would have to talk about the sadness if it kept looming about.

"You do have a point. I was adopted so was Izzy." Giovanni muttered, picking up his spork to dig into the mashed potatoes on his tray.

Fiona felt realization hit her like a ton of bricks. She had been dipping her roll into mashed potatoes, taking small bites from her delicious, mixed collaboration. She stopped eating mid-way, "Izzy? I knew a boy with that name. His parents were going to give him up, but we can't know the same Izzy."

Giovanni rose an eyebrow as Sonya looked intrigued. He was unsure of why Fiona thought such an idea impossible. He leaned forward, wondering if he should speak the last name of

Izzy.

"Fiona, nothing is impossible." Sonya disagreed as Fiona shook her head in disbelief.

"He set his brother on fire so his parents wanted to be rid of a serial killer in the making." Giovanni spoke the word for word truth of what Izzy eventually confessed to him, watching panic mixed with alarm cause Fiona's eyes to widen.

Fiona shook her head with silent tears, beginning to stream down her cheeks. "No, you can't possibly know that!"

Giovanni didn't get a chance to comment when the hysterical Fiona Calvert got up to take her tray and leave. He was officially confused. Why would someone like Fiona be in denial over what little he knew to be true?

Sonya sighed, but remained by Giovanni's side. She spoke up in order to answer the questions running through Giovanni's head. "Fiona had been dating Oliver Sprouse for a few years AKA the older brother of your beloved Isaiah."

Harsh Truth

"I still don't see what Fiona has to do with any of this." Giovanni said, casually shrugging. His full attention was on Sonya nor could he clear his head after that day at lunch. He nor Sonya had seen Fiona for the last five days after the revelation of who she was to Izzy and what she meant to the younger lad. He was concerned for Fiona, but even more concerned for Izzy who seemed to have recoiled even more into himself.

Sonya had told Giovanni she would meet up with him over the phone. She wanted to walk to school with him while promising to bring cappuccinos. She had gotten his proper order, smirking to herself upon finally getting Gio to open up go her.

Of course, they had been talking on the phone every night since he was at the Hemingway household. Both parties grew warmer, feeling good about their late night chats.

Giovanni had hope for the first time since the orphanage. He got along with Caleb as well as Nazz and Shua. He wasn't quite comfortable with calling them mom and dad nor did they mind.

He wasn't sure if he would ever be able to call them parents.

"The full story from what I gather is a lot more complicated." Sonya said, nonchalantly shrugging before adding, "Than what either of us are aware of."

"How did you two become friends?" Giovanni asked Sonya as they opted to sit on swings at the park. He wanted to meet up with Sonya before they found their way to school. He liked her more than any girl he had liked prior nor did he want a moment to go to waste.

"Fiona wasn't speaking to anyone when I first came here. She was actually shut off while avoiding those as best as she could around her. It's not like she doesn't get hate by former friends." Sonya informed Giovanni in one take. She sipped her pumpkin spice cappuccino before sitting on a swing.

Giovanni copied her action while thankful for a pumpkin spice flavored cappuccino this go around. He was content, "She was a loner?"

"Oh, there is no 'was' considering Fiona still is a loner. I'm the one person she chose to be open with. She accidentally bumped into me, spilling lukewarm coffee on me which is how we met. She profusely apologized as if accidents don't happen." Sonya whimsically responded like she was in a dream upon recounting their meeting.

"Do you not know much about her relationship with Oliver Sprouse?" Giovanni curiously pried. He didn't want to have to bring Izzy into the mix if he could avoid it. He wasn't sure how Izzy would feel about Fiona Calvert or what tragedy she might ensure on his behalf.

"No, her relationship with the Sprouse boy was before I came along. I don't think she ever mourned him." Sonya released a sad sigh, averting her gray eyes to the beautiful, fresh, cut, vibrant green grass.

Giovanni nodded, taking another swig of the seasonal holiday caffeinated beverage. "Thank you again for this, Soy."

Sonya turned red via a blush on account of him saying her nickname. She didn't mind Giovanni calling her Soy, but she always scolded Fiona for it. She looked to Fiona like she was the sister she never had upon growing up. "You should thank my parents. They own the Soy Bean Latte Café."

"Why did they choose to go with such a long winded name?" Giovanni playfully asks, smiling over at the girl who mirrored his own smile.

Sonya sighed, gingerly toying with the base of her neck where a light pink locket sat on a silver chain. "My father made a joke about it being geared towards me to run—someday. I wouldn't mind owning the café one day."

"What about your mother?" Giovanni curiously inquires, lifting an eyebrow while keeping his silver gray eyes glued to the beautiful girl in his view.

Sonya shrugs, "My mom is secretive. None of us know what she does. She could be a serial killer—burying bodies in the backyard without our knowledge."

"You're kidding, right?" Giovanni almost choked to death on the cappuccino. He clutched it tighter, praying Sonya was giving off some humorous vibes.

"Afraid not. Shouldn't we get to school?" Sonya spoke only to bolt to her feet. She patiently waits for Giovanni with furrowed eyebrows.

Giovanni copied her action, gulping down the entire Styrofoam cup of light brown liquid. "We should get to school, but where has your best friend been hiding?"

"I'm not sure. I think I know where we can look, but I can't afford to let my grades slip." Sonya said, gently tugging on his hand. She nodded in the direction of Orlando Adams High School, groaning at the length of the name.

Giovanni almost felt right at home. He half smiled at how close he had become with the brown complected girl who already had his heart. "Who said anything about, we?"

"You were the one asking about someone you don't know. Thought you were a concerned friend." Sonya remarked, upturning her palms in a shrug. She began to exit the park with Giovanni.

Giovanni sighed as he walked by her side to school. He frowned as they went along, "I am a concerned friend. How are you even sure she's still alive?"

Sonya went rigid in her spot, turning to look at Giovanni with wide eyes. "I didn't even think twice about that. What kind of friend, am I?"

Giovanni shook his head, "It's not your fault. You didn't—"

"You don't understand." Sonya ominously spoke, cutting him off. She left him standing there, scurrying away from him— in the search for her friend.

Giovanni truly didn't understand. He was back to square one where he first started. He stuck his hands into the pockets of his pants, mildly confused about his crush. He truly did want to help Sonya with Fiona, but how? He didn't know either of the girls well enough.

Anger Management

"Gio, why bring your problems to me? I can't help you." Caleb spoke in a bit of a growl. He wasn't adjusting so well to the new high school. He thought people would flock around him like he actually mattered.

Giovanni bawled up his fists, "You were the one telling people about me being an orphan. I don't yearn for people to know unless I want them to know."

"Sorry, bro, but I have my reasoning." Caleb said, cooling down. He was doing his best to get a handle on his anger. His temper had been out of control recently nor did he enjoy the untamed embers burning inside.

Giovanni sighed, leaning on the cherry red oak dresser. The bedroom was decked out in all red as if Caleb was a Gryffindor, "What's wrong with you, Blossom? You seem different."

"What's the point in saying? I heard you made new friends. Good for you." Caleb sadly smiled, trying to be happy for his adopted brother. He was leaning on the edge of his queen sized bed, coveted in dark red satin sheets.

Giovanni frowned, "I haven't seen my new friends in a good week. However, I did befriend two girls."

Caleb grew interested, straightening his stiff posture. "You said girls?"

Giovanni vigorously nodded his head, "Yep."

A soft knock came on the bedroom door of Caleb who shouted for whomever was on the other side to enter. He wasn't in the best mood, doing his best to remain open to Gio and Izzy. He sighed while Izzy soon appeared in his doorway.

Izzy appeared to be fidgeting with his fingers. He had this ever-present pout plastered across his tanned features. He looked like he wanted to say something only for Caleb to speak up, beating him to the punch.

"What are the names of these two girls you supposedly befriended?" Caleb curiously rattled off which really captured the attention of Izzy.

Izzy furrowed his eyebrows, wondering what the ginger was on about. He had a dreadful feeling. His heart fluttered beneath his left ribcage.

Giovanni cleared his throat, shaking his head. He couldn't bring up the topic of Fiona Calvert in front of Izzy, could he? "I'd rather not say."

Caleb saw the steely gleam in Giovanni's eyes, making him wonder what he did wrong. His eyes drifted to Izzy, "Isaiah is old enough to know about girls. I think. Given his attitude—his mind might differ."

Giovanni shook his head, "This doesn't revolve around Izzy."

"Then, what are their names?" Caleb pressed, gaining a scowl from Giovanni. He was aware that Gio wanted him to knock it off.

"Forget I mentioned anything about girls. I have something

more urgent to discuss with you." Giovanni said as a frown placated Izzy's face. He was causing suspicious to develop within Izzy and Caleb on his behalf.

Izzy knew of only one girl that he yearned to know the whereabouts of. He said nothing to elaborate on the topic of what guys generally fancied. He glanced from Giovanni to Caleb in evident wonderment.

"What's more pressing than girls?" Caleb furrowed his dark red eyebrows at Giovanni's question.

"Green flames." Giovanni replied in a two worded, short response. He didn't want to dive into the over exhausted detail, aware that his newly adopted brothers would catch on.

Caleb gingerly nodded, "Green flames. I have black and Izzy has blue. All three of us are cursed."

Giovanni dropped his shoulders, "Flames are meant to cleanse which is something a lot of people don't understand. How can that make us cursed?"

Caleb once more nodded. His mind began to wander as he mulled over the information brought to light. He stroked his chin while continuing to lean on his dresser.

Izzy wasn't too pleased about how willing the ignorant ginger was to tell secrets no one wanted him to spill. He shot Caleb a chilly glare.

"Okay, but how are colored flames different from just being a regular firestarter?" Caleb inquired, also wanting to know why they were any different.

Izzy seemed to have some insight on the subject, "I don't think it's necessarily a curse placed on families like it's to be believed by some people. It's so easy to twist what someone else says with no proof."

"Isaiah is one smart cookie." Caleb voices being half sarcastic while trying not to further egg the younger boy on. He called the boy by his given name since Izzy didn't want Caleb using any of his nicknames. He figured it was best to not push him over the edge.

"How would you know so much, Izzy? We haven't heard from you since your silent retreat into yourself." Giovanni ponders aloud, slightly surprised by the straightforwardness of Izzy.

"I found this brown leather book, lying in the middle of my bed. I'm fairly certain someone gifted it to me. It distinguishes the differences of the colored flames in the book." Izzy rattled off in explanation. He thought nothing of it, casually shrugging.

"So, what are the differences between our colored flames versus the natural flames?" Caleb asked, getting down to business. He knew they didn't have time for games nor did he want to play games.

"My blue flames are to cleanse the world of the sinners. The black flames are to help control the darkness in the good. The green flames can be healing, but they aren't as strong." Izzy swiftly informed his brothers, giving a nonchalant shrug.

Caleb averted his brown eyes to the red carpet where they were darting all over in his venture to process the revelation. He was making sense of what little they learned from the eighteen year old, "Who would leave you such a book?"

"My guardian angel. How should I know?" Izzy sarcastically remarked, shrugging to showcase his uncertainty. At the time, he genuinely didn't know.

Caleb sighed, "Whatever, Isaiah! Go play with your... whatever little boys do."

Izzy scowled at Caleb. He was once again being underestimated by people older than him. He internally groaned, wishing they would listen to him. He disliked being ignored as much as he disliked being thought of a child, especially when he was of age.

Three Plus Two

Caleb had started his own session of smoking cigarettes. He was attempting to light a cigarette when he noticed her. He forgot what he was trying to do as he shook his head at the sight of the forgotten girl, "Sonya?"

The girl tensed in her spot. She was idly chatting away with her best friend. She hadn't heard or seen him since the prep school she wanted to forget. "Caleb Hemingway."

Caleb didn't let the icy chill in her tone go unnoticed. "Soy, you were my best girl!"

Sonya scoffed, turning about face with Fiona. "Caleb, I've done told you. An ignoramus is not my type."

Caleb rolled his eyes. He shot a smile at the best friend of Sonya, "Who's your lovely friend?"

"Caleb, this is Fiona. Fiona, this is the ginger I told you about." Sonya made short introductions, unable to stand it any longer. She thought Caleb was an okay guy at first—when she thought she knew him at their prep school. The real world not only showed Sonya who she was, but who she wasn't.

Fiona smirked, "He's the ginger who sold Giovanni out to the whole school then?"

Caleb tensed, cupping his ear. He was praying his ears were playing tricks on him. "Giovanni, who?"

"Hey, ladies! I've been looking everywhere for...Caleb?" Giovanni eagerly chirped, beginning to deflate when he caught sight of the rich boy. He had two cappuccinos in hand for both of the girls he had become good friends with.

Caleb's jaw fell agape, opting to feign shock, "Giovanni, Fiona, Sonya. Wow! Who could have guessed?"

"These were the girls I mentioned having befriended." Giovanni muttered, gingerly handing the cappuccinos to each girl.

"Yeah, well, this was the ginger I mentioned selling you out about being an orphan." Fiona chirped, sipping the peppermint flavored cappuccino.

Giovanni briefly smiled at Sonya before catching the scowl dancing across Caleb's face. "What, Caleb?"

Caleb folded his arms to his chest, shaking his head at Giovanni. "I should have known you were only being friendly towards me to steal, Soy from me. She was the one good thing in my life."

"I was never yours to steal." Sonya stuck up for herself, hating how Caleb talked like she wasn't present. She had a mind of her own just like him and everyone else did.

Caleb felt a sting in his heart via her words. "I always did think you were beautiful. I wasn't as ignorant as you thought. I was just lonely."

"So, whatever happened to your best boyfriend?" Fiona asked in a snort. She didn't buy the grief of Caleb Hemingway for a minute. She knew how rich guys appeared acting as if they were the victims for having money.

"How would you know about Rory? Soy, you didn't spill my secrets…" Caleb tried to make sense of the betrayal. He went on to add, "Rory wasn't my boyfriend. He was my best friend—the closest I ever had to a brother figure in my life."

"Was?" Sonya sadly asked, having once known Rory Morrison. She too had been the best of friends with the other prep school boy. She thought Rory was sweet, truly rooting for the blonde.

"He's dead, but thank you for being the biggest bitch on the planet." Caleb snarled, shoving past the three traitors in order to head inside the red, brick building. He knew it was going to be the same old same for him. He hardly had any friends at his old school nor had anything changed for him. He was going to be the odd man out forever.

"Someone needs to take a chill pill." A female voice suddenly cooed, speaking from beside the ginger. She had witnessed the ordeal with the redhead and group of three. She took an interest in the pale skinned, brown eyed male.

Caleb shot the girl a glare until his brown eyes landed on her. He scratched the top of his head, "Who the fuck are you?"

"I love a man who cusses. I'm Melanie Stefani, but I prefer Mel." She softly quipped, grinning like the Cheshire cat as she extended a caramel complected hand towards him. Her eyes were honey colored with blood red curls falling loosely down her shoulders. She was about five foot three with a curvy figure to her.

She was wearing blue, low rise jeans showcasing her abdomen. The soft pink long sleeve turtle neck she wore was cut to show her midriff much like the jeans hugging her curves in all the right places. She was a busty eighteen year old with quite the mix of her heritage.

66

"I'm…" Caleb trailed off, forgetting his name the moment his hand made contact with hers. His anger for Sonya, Fiona, and Giovanni washed away as a soft smile graced his milky features.

Melanie chuckled at his sudden loss of memory. She was patient while he searched his brain for his own name. "You're the transfer from Bluejay Prep."

He softly smiled at how she knew what she knew. "Yes, um, my name is Caleb Hemingway."

"What a sound name!" Melanie beamed, gesturing to Spanish class. She went on to playfully add in a giggle. "I don't think you take Español though."

Caleb tilted his head sideways at the short girl, "What is Español?"

Melanie shook her head, "Español is Spanish. Duh!"

Caleb vigorously shook his head to kill the cobwebs. When did he become stupid around girls suddenly? He had known the Spanish word for the language. He didn't know why he was acting a fool, "Mel, I'm sorry. I'm usually smart about these things."

Melanie watched the ginger leave the classroom as she gave him the tiniest of waves. A small smile slid onto her caramel features as Caleb walked off. She was happy to have introduced herself.

Caleb had never felt dumber. It had never been easy for him to make a fool of himself. How could he start acting so foolish in front of Melanie Stefani? He didn't even know the gorgeous girl aside from that she takes Spanish class.

Stand Up

Caleb had opted to sit alone during lunch. He wanted to give Giovanni his time in the spotlight so he made sure to take a seat at the back. He was also hoping to see the beautiful Melanie Stefani a second time. He hadn't seen her after the incident in Spanish class which didn't sit too well within him. He was slurping down a small carton of chocolate milk while he waited.

What he didn't expect to hear was people bullying those around him. His eyebrows shot up as he overheard a guy, making cow noises at a girl. He wasn't about to continue sitting idly by to hear the jerks doing it. He took a deep breath, getting up as he threw his tray away. He wouldn't be able to eat anymore after the commotion he heard.

"You're an ugly skank that nobody would want!" Adam Smith poked a finger at his latest victim. He was the popular jock everyone loved to flock around.

Caleb wasn't a part of the flock. He shoved Adam out of the way, shooting a glare of daggers at the dark haired male. "It's not nice to make fun of someone!"

Adam snorted, shoving Caleb to the ground like the busty mixed girl he had moments prior to Caleb jumping in to aide her. "Wow, would you like to be her boyfriend?"

Caleb had yet to glimpse the girl they were making fun of. His fingers clenched into fists. "Would you like to eat heat for lunch?"

Adam harshly gulped upon the black flames emanating from the palms of Caleb. He began to silently freak out as did the group of popular jerks around him. "Fuck! Never mind! He's cursed!"

With those words, the popular kids began to scramble away. The jerks at Orlando Adams High left him on the ground with the unseen girl. He wished the age would be brought to eighteen for people to leave high school. Instead of nineteen being the required age—made no sense to him.

Caleb felt the urge to go after the kids, and rip their bodies to pieces for bullying an innocent. His nostrils were flaring as his eyes almost matched the color of his flames. He was about to spring to his feet when the soft, warm hand of a familiar female was on his shoulder. He began to visibly relax with a sense of calm washing over his brooding features. His flames were tamed as he twisted to look at the one person he had grown to fancy so quickly.

"Mel?" Caleb inquired, frowning as he saw the tears, staining her caramel complected features. He used a thumb to wipe the stray tears away, stirring comfort in him to know he found his connection. He got to his feet, extending a hand to the girl he liked.

Melanie was a bit skeptical to take his hand for fear of judgement. She took his hand anyway when she saw the uncaring gleam in his eye. The uncaring gleam was meant for those who thought they were better than anyone else which was something she rather enjoyed about the boy in her view. "Gracias, Caleb."

"I'm sorry they were making fun of you for no reason. I think they're just jealous." Caleb grumbled, leaving the lunchroom with Melanie next to him.

Melanie shyly smiled at him, "I think that they're just jealous because they don't eat enough."

"That, and they couldn't pull off the beautiful curvy figure God gave you." Caleb softly grinned, meaning every word of what he said. He wanted to wrap an arm around her to bring Melanie closer to him, but would she be alright with the action? He was taller than her.

"Don't make me blush. You can't mean that." Melanie said with her face turning a cherry shade of red. She wanted to refrain from blushing, but with Caleb—it was no use.

"What? A guy isn't allowed to like someone for their personality anymore? If so, the world is one messed up place." Caleb said, hating the notion. He scoffed at the thought, rolling his brown eyes.

Melanie felt even dumber for jumping to conclusions on his behalf, "I'm sorry, Caleb. I've just never had any guy truly take an interest in me."

"Other than for sex?" Caleb asked, already understanding what she was implying. He didn't like the pained expression that followed his question. He used his fingertips to gently touch her chin so their eyes locked, "Mel, Sweetheart, you are not an object. You are a beautiful human being who loves herself, but who also has her flaws."

Melanie felt a smile creep onto her face, knowing what Caleb was getting at. She had one ex-boyfriend who never got her like Caleb somehow managed to. "You also have flaws, twig!"

"Ouch!" Caleb said, removing his fingers from her chin. He feigned, placing a hand over his heart in a playful manner. "Twig?"

Melanie smirked which helped to shift the mood of Caleb to a much better one. "It's my nickname for you!"

"You could always call me, Blossom." Caleb said, causing Melanie to shake her head in disagreement at him. A light frown tugged his lips downwards.

"I think I like Twig better." Melanie confessed, gaining an annoyed eye roll from him. She added as an afterthought, "Blossom makes you sound like a Powderpuff Girl—I hate those cartoons."

Caleb sighed, "Fine. You win, Mel, but I won't enjoy the name calling."

Melanie nearly frowned, "I thought you loved your body?"

"Who in this age truly loves their own body?" Caleb challenged, furrowing his eyebrows at her. His question caused food for thought to enter her brain. He was glad to have Melanie by his side—through and through.

$\mathcal{L.O.V.E.}$

Izzy Sprouse was beyond hysterical. He took to the library to eat his lunch. He truly did hate high school nor did he think anything would make it better. He couldn't eat as his fingers were intertwined in his dark brown curls upon his head. His elbows were on the table as invisible tears swelled at the back of his eyes.

His brothers were already finding their connection. He knew all about the connection. He had it with the one person he was sure he would never see again. There was more to his story than what he let those around him choose to believe. He had been in love with someone he could never have or at least— that's what people would say if they knew the truth.

Izzy's heart was in shambles. He didn't think he would live again until he tried to sit in the lunchroom one afternoon. His cerulean blue eyes scanned the cafeteria to sit with Giovanni or Caleb even if he was still on bitter terms for whatever reason with the ginger. He inhaled deeply, coming across a sight for sore eyes when he finally spotted Giovanni. His eyes narrowed into a squint; mostly one of disbelief as he saw her.

For him— it was like looking at a ghost. He grew speechless as he stood in the doorway of the double doors of the cafeteria. He saw just how unhappy she looked, making him wonder if she would blame him for what took place. He immediately paled, knowing he would not be able to talk to her for fear of what might transpire. He was about to make a quick exit when Giovanni caught sight of him.

"Izzy! Come on over!" Giovanni happily shouted, waving the brunette boy over. He didn't notice the tense up of Fiona who froze mid-whatever she was doing.

Izzy saw her tense at the mention of his name. He shook his head at Giovanni who refused to let him slip away. He couldn't confront what was past, could he? He was about to find out.

Giovanni wouldn't take no for an answer so he got up to drag Izzy over to the table consisting of him, Sonya, and Fiona. Earlier on, he would have left Izzy to do his own thing. He was tired of not being able to speak to Izzy without the eighteen year old aware of said truth.

"No! I don't—" Izzy tried to protest, but it was already too late. He was aggressively dragged over to the table where Giovanni had been sitting with the two girls. To say, he didn't recognize Fiona Calvert would be the understatement of the year; he didn't know her friend.

"Ladies, this is Isaiah Sprouse or Izzy for short." Giovanni stated, slinging an arm around Izzy's shoulders, making him uncomfortable. He went on to add. "Izzy, this is Sonya Addison and my other good friend is Fiona Calvert."

Fiona was reluctant to let her gaze meet the cerulean blue eyes of Izzy. She remained not only haunted by his eyes, but the softness of his lips. She could never forget the gentle touch he bestowed upon her even when she tried. She had never felt anything so sweet with her former boyfriend, but she willed herself to love Oliver more than she could ever hope to.

Izzy saw grief and happiness shine in her striking emerald green eyes. His breath got stuck in the back of his throat as if they were meeting all over again. He opened his mouth to speak, but no words came out when he was too entranced by the brunette female he had missed. His bitterness and anger from before had washed away like he was seeing the light for the first time. For a minute, he grew scared that it was all a dream he would wake up from.

"Hi, Izzy. It's nice to meet you." Sonya perked up, giving the brunette lad a light wave of her hand to make sure Izzy saw her acknowledgement. She tried not to smirk due to the smitten look on his face that was directed towards Fiona.

Izzy shook his head in order to get himself to come out of his trance. His blue eyes met the light gray of Sonya who liked soft pink sweaters with ripped blue jeans. "Hi, Sonya, it's nice to meet you. Gio mentioned befriending two girls. I didn't know who he could have meant—prior."

Giovanni pursed his lips, motioning for Izzy to sit down beside him. "Join us. I have missed you. Our conversations got lost in the echo."

"I can't. I have to study. I'm sorely lacking in getting good grades this year." Izzy said, feeling ashamed since he didn't think Fiona would take too kindly to his presence. He just didn't want to make her uncomfortable. He had known what Oliver meant to Fiona—and not what Izzy meant to her.

"Well, Fiona is failing too. We could always form a study group." Sonya softly chirped, gaining a scorned look from Fiona. She shot her best friend an innocent look. She could see what

74

clearly Izzy was missing.

Izzy wasn't sure if he should be relieved or surprised. He fumbled with his backpack straps, shifting from one foot to the other. He was standing at the end of the table, feeling completely out of place. "I definitely think I should—"

"Move out of the way, loser!" The voice of Adam Smith yelled, slamming directly into Izzy Sprouse. His nostrils were flaring as snot seeped from the loser's nose. He caused Izzy to tense, becoming nauseated by the bully.

Izzy scowled as he was interrupted. His temper rose as he made contact with the floor. His food flew all over the place. "Get off of me, sicko! What's your deal?"

Adam didn't like people assuming he was a sicko. He was ready to give Izzy a knockout punch which is when he raised a fist to the boy. He would enjoy the blood gushing from the eighteen year old nuisance.

Dark Horse

Fiona rolled her eyes. She bolted from her spot, yanking Adam off of Izzy. She angrily shoved the popular boy to the floor—opposite Izzy. "Why don't you go pick on someone who looks like you?"

"You don't scare me!" Adam growled at the brunette who wasn't phased by him. He was trying to be scary, reminding Fiona of someone else.

Fiona crossed her arms, standing straight in front of Izzy so he wasn't in harm's way. She always felt the need to watch out for him so when the opportunity arose she would. She wasn't as mad at him which is what Izzy kept assuming.

Izzy's palms were engulfed by blue flames. He tried to cool down, recalling where he was. His heart was beating ferociously in his chest as Fiona stood up for him. Her voice made him want to melt on the spot.

"You don't scare me, Smith! Get lost before I make you lost!" Fiona practically growled at the popular boy. Her eyes remained steely, watching the school bully.

Adam's eyes caught sight of the cursed Izzy Sprouse which sent him running from the cafeteria. He briefly threw a glance over his shoulder to make sure he wasn't being chased.

Fiona smirked, turning around in order to crouch down to lend Izzy a hand up from the cafeteria floor. She rolled her green eyes at the dust littering the floor, semi unsurprised.

Izzy didn't hesitate to let Fiona help him up. A frown placated his features as he opted to sit down beside Giovanni across from his crush. He felt the need to ask Fiona why she stuck up for him, but he let the question fall from his mind as he eyed his messy long sleeve shirt.

"The janitor is not going to be happy." Sonya said, gaining a scoff from Fiona. She too wasn't happy about the idea of fighting let alone Adam Smith being able to roam free to do what he wants.

"I'll talk to him about having Adam help since he created the disaster." Fiona pipes up, grunting as she began to tug off her black knit sweater. She was sure she could get Adam involved in helping the janitor.

"Fiona, what are you doing?" Sonya hissed as her best friend stripped in front of everyone. Her eyes bulged from her eye sockets, hoping the nineteen year old would come off of her weirdness.

Giovanni almost choked on his milk. He cleared his throat, attempting not to die. He liked calcium, but not that much.

Fiona always came prepared. She had a snug fitting, blue tank top on underneath her sweater. She held her black knit sweater towards Izzy who was still in shock, "This should fit you."

Sonya felt relief stir in her heart upon realizing Fiona had more clothing on underneath. "Isn't it freezing out, Fiona?"

"My trusty orange flannel is tucked into my backpack. I need to get to my locker before class, but it is freezing out." Fiona answered the question last, beaming at her best friend. She never failed to be prepared.

Izzy gingerly took the sweater, anxiously pulling it on over his head. It was medium sized so it hung a little loose on him, but he didn't mind. He felt safe, and at home in the sweater. "Thank you, Fiona."

Fiona softly smiled at him as goosebumps littered her skin from the way he said her name. She shrugged, "I like to help those deserving of it."

Izzy rose an eyebrow at her sentiment. He wondered if the few times they kissed meant anything to her. He felt utterly ridiculous after her revelation. It was then that he realized he could go for a nice nap.

"Izz, what's wrong?" Giovanni asked from next to him. He had noticed the sadness erupt in Izzy the moment Fiona mentioned she liked helping people. He sort of understood what the younger boy was going through.

Izzy said nothing as a pout took hold of his features. He was ready to lay his head down until Fiona spoke some more. He couldn't help, but to listen to her. He had been captivated by the older girl from day one.

"He could be hungry. His lunch went to waste. Here, I don't mind sharing." Fiona said, scooting her tray closer to Izzy. She sported a small smile, directed at Izzy.

Izzy wrinkled his nose, trying to figure her out. He knew Fiona wasn't one to share her food. He wordlessly took a tater tot, plopping it into his mouth. As he began to chew, he realized just how hungry he had been.

Fiona didn't eat too much for fear of people watching her eat. She didn't even like standing in the lunch line. What made all the difference was how she had friends. Otherwise, she wouldn't eat lunch or breakfast at school. She hardly got dinner at home so she would be lucking out if she missed the school food.

Sonya always did go easy on Fiona which is why she always paid for their coffee. She knew some of what the home life for Fiona was like. She cut her light gray eyes to Fiona after casting a glance at Izzy.

"Thank you." Izzy gently replied, frowning at how he barely left her anything. A slither of guilt began to swarm in his heart. Was he really that selfish?

"We're good." Fiona said as if she hadn't just helped the boy out tremendously in one day. She held no grudges even with what Izzy did to Oliver. She could have told anyone it was an accident, given she knew Izzy.

"Isn't that Caleb?" Giovanni suddenly asked, having caught sight of Caleb walking out with the new girl. He seemed lighter as they clung to one another.

"Yeah, he's with Melanie Stefani. She's not really new, but Adam Smith has decided to start bullying her. So, she's fairly new to some of us." Sonya replied in a gentle whisper. She hung her head in a bout of defeat.

"She takes Spanish Class. She comes from an Italian-Mexican bloodline. People don't understand it, but who cares?" Fiona said, shrugging as she eyed the pair who were already out of sight. She thought those two looked quite cozy, walking in sync.

"Apparently, Adam Smith cares." Giovanni stated as Sonya rolls her eyes. He was just taking mental notes of what he bore witness to.

"He only cares about bullying people and popularity." Sonya

corrected, popping the last tater tot into her mouth. She was about done with lunch.

Meant to Be

Izzy was sitting crisscross applesauce on his bed. His eyes were shut while he thought solely of Fiona Calvert. He missed the soft warmth of her lips pressed to his. His mind kept returning to what he thought were forgotten memories. His bedroom was decked out in all dark blue coloring which made no sense to him.

The queen sized bed he slept in was coveted in dark blue satin sheets. The oak dresser was also dark blue with walls, and carpet to match. He guessed that whoever decorated made a lucky guess on his part.

He inhaled deeply as he meditated. He wanted to throw away all the bad energy in order to be able to breathe in the good energy. As he sat upon his bed— a shuffling noise caused his ears to perk up, but he didn't pay it any mind; at first.

Fiona grimaced, having gingerly opened the window. She landed swiftly in the middle of his bedroom. Her hands were on her hips as she bore her orange coated flannel jacket over a soft blue tee shirt. She smirked at seeing Izzy meditate on his bed as she slunk over to stand in front of him. Her hands came to rest on her waistline with a smirk becoming visible on her lips.

His eyes shot open causing him to gasp at the sudden appearance of Fiona. "Fiona, what are you doing here?"

"I wanted you to know, I don't blame you. I'm not stupid." Fiona rattled off in explanation to Izzy. Her words were true. She didn't lay blame to Izzy for the death of his brother and her ex-boyfriend.

"It was an accident." Izzy said, feeling guilt tug at his heartstrings. He could have done without her reminding him. Some relief did stir in his heart by her confession.

Fiona nodded, choosing to plop down on the foot of his bed beside him. Her eyes met his in a sympathetic glance, "I just told you, I'm not daft."

Izzy frowned. "I don't know what else you expect me to say."

Fiona groaned. "I thought you should also know, I left the brown leather book for you. I knew about the curses on certain families."

Izzy scowled, twisting to look at the guilt ridden female. "Were you never going to tell me?"

Fiona held sorrow in her striking green eyes. "I was going to tell you that night. Of course, everything bad happened before I could reach you. I went looking for you when you ran away, but I couldn't find you."

Izzy furrowed his eyebrows, "If you're the one who left me the book then how come you didn't—"

"Don't ask questions that will harm the soul. I have my reasoning for what I've done." Fiona said, quick to interrupt him. She gave a slight shake of her head. She knew he had his own reasoning for what he had done too—even when it was an accident.

Izzy sighed, still not making sense of it all. "You didn't come find me."

"Why would I?" Fiona asked, quirking an eyebrow up at the boy. She knew what she mentioned prior, but she couldn't search for Izzy after she discovered he ran away. She hadn't known he had been in an orphanage. She only just got word of Izzy being adopted into a new home which is when she left the book.

Izzy didn't like her question. He could have sworn she felt the same way he did. He averted his gaze to the blue carpet of his bedroom, "It doesn't matter anyhow. What took you so long to actually realize I was still here?"

"I was grieving, Isaiah. I don't expect you to understand the turmoil I was going through. Of course, I didn't think... however, I was wrong." Fiona gently spoke, further confusing the curly haired boy. She had grieved Oliver—what he could have been had he yearned to change his behavior; not who he had been.

"I still wish I could have changed that night. He found out about our kiss, and threatened me. He even went so far as to—" Izzy began to whimper as his breathing grew shallow with an offbeat heart. He stopped speaking mid-sentence.

Fiona knew what he meant. She sighed, choosing to place a hand on his shoulder. Her touch was as gentle as his lips had been when he first kissed her. She shook her head to clear the image as he began to slowly relax under her touch, "We all wish we could change certain things. I'm sorry. I feel like it was my fault."

"Did you tell him?" Izzy asked, glancing over at Fiona. He was curious as Fiona looked all the more guilty. He couldn't blame her—he supposed.

"I couldn't not. He was my boyfriend. I didn't think his anger was that bad. I'm sorry. Please don't hate me!" Fiona gently remarked, removing her hand from his shoulder. She felt ten times worse knowing it was all her fault, but she didn't want to have to lie to her boyfriend.

Izzy sighed, seeing the grief and guilt blended into her gaze. He couldn't blame her. If he had been in a relationship with someone else during that time; he wouldn't lie to his significant other either. His shoulders dropped as he softly spoke, "I don't hate you, Fiona. I never could."

Fiona yawned, half smiling at the blue eyed boy. "I never could hate you either, Isaiah."

Izzy mirrored her smile, locking eyes with her. "Did you love Oliver?"

Fiona felt her heart crack at the question. Her nerves twisted her tongue. Should she even answer the question with honesty? If she did then she would be selling herself short. "I wanted to love Oliver which is why I didn't break it off with him. He needed someone in order to cope."

"You've always been so kind to me. Why?" Izzy curiously wondered, catching the warmth in her striking green eyes on his behalf.

"Let's just say, I know what it's like being abused and needing someone to be kind." Fiona muttered, fidgeting with her fingers. She harshly gulped, before releasing a shaky breath.

Lord of Chaos

Benjamin stood there with a smirk plastered across his fair features. All his life he got what he wanted by taking whatever it is he wanted. He didn't care for the well being of others nor did he have to take a dark turn. He was in the Orlando Jay graveyard where the fog was rolling in. His light green eyes, turned entirely dark as his fingernails grew longer.

His fingernails grew to be yellow while becoming elongated. He knew the untamed, cursed families were real. He knew the time for revenge was winding down. His eyes were on the gravestone he was standing over. He had dug up the place someone was meant to be buried, but never had been.

He held up his right wrist over the grave, using a fingernail to draw blood. He maliciously grinned as the blood dripped into the cracked, dirt of the Earth. He would be happy when he summoned his lord of chaos. He might have been in cahoots with the devil, but he didn't need many people to know. He had been in search of the cursed three who would be the sacrificial lamb to bring forth his lord of chaos in an actual body.

"I summon thee!" Benjamin growled into the eerie silence of the dead of night. He welcomed the anger, the hatred, and the negative power into his veins. It was him after all, smirking as he did his ritual.

A creature in all black appeared. It looked as one would expect— dead with the smell of rotting flesh. It did no good to glimpse the lord of chaos without shivering due to fear and disgust. Some people had fear while others lacked the emotion that could save or destroy.

Benjamin didn't inch closer, instead instinctively moving away like a normal person would. His dark eyes widened in an even more gleeful manner. "My lord—"

"No!" The lord of chaos growled at Benjamin in interruption. He wagged a finger at the green eyed boy, "I don't think so."

"What do you want me to call you then?" Benjamin asked, growing confused. He rose an eyebrow, parting his lips while watching his lord. He should have summoned him sooner yet had been unable to—right timing and all that jazz.

"I shall go by the human name of Jason." The lord of chaos replied, further confusing the evil male. He couldn't just be seen with Benjamin Calvert and be called—lord of chaos.

"Okay, but why?" Benjamin did not get it. When did he ever get anything anyone said to him? He wasn't the sharpest tool in the shed.

"It's an undercover gig until I get what I came for." Jason said, causing Benjamin to nod his head. He was waiting for Benjamin to bow down, kneeling before him.

"I found the cursed three like we discussed." Benjamin offered the news, baffling his lord of chaos. He was sure the being would be happy with his discovery.

"What makes you think there's only three? I hate to break

86

this to you, but the curse isn't limited to three." Jason revealed causing Benjamin to scrunch up his face. He was knowledgeable unlike his accomplice.

"Are you saying there's more than three?" Benjamin inquired, shaking his head. He almost lost the darkness in his eyes. His sacrifice of Rory Morrison had been to bring his lord of chaos to the mortal realm.

Jason gave a slight nod. "Yes, there's always more. People miscalculate fire as a curse, but I'm not stupid. It cleanses the soul."

"How many will we need for you to gain a mortal body?" Benjamin inquired as his curiosity continued to grow. He did a double take while his boss seemed ever-thoughtful.

Jason released a throaty growl. "I only need three. The old saying always talks about stuff happening in threes. Nor is this any exception."

"I have one, but where one is—" Benjamin speaks, clamping his mouth down shut when he kicks around a sentence that makes sense. His eyes widen as he adds, "Others should be. Didn't you say those with fire can't survive without the sibling bond?"

"Correct, but guys don't feel. So, how in the world could your one bond with others?" Jason snarled, causing Benjamin to scratch the back of his neck. He was confused about the words of Benjamin, having heard no sane explanation from the man.

Benjamin knew how close Caleb Hemingway had been with the likes of Rory Morrison. He knew they were the best of friends, but even friendship held some type of emotional bond to it. "I wouldn't say that. Caleb was a pretty emotional guy."

Jason turned towards Benjamin like he had grown an extra head. Why did Benjamin say was as if the redhead had died?

He was assuming this Caleb character was one of the currently 'cursed three' in existence.

The rotting smell hit the nostrils of Benjamin causing him to grunt in disgust. His eyes burned just from the raunchy, stank smell coming from off the dead being. His lord of chaos sure could use a good wash. "My lord—"

"What did I say?" Jason growled, wanting to throttle the demonic boy. His tone and eyes held a sharp glare in the direction of Benjamin.

Benjamin cleared his throat, inhaling sharply. "Sorry, Jason, I'm fairly certain he would have bonded with others. I haven't figured out who quite yet."

"Well, do so, and don't let me down." Jason growled, backing away from Benjamin. He was ready to be alone to his own thoughts. He needed to gain as much energy from the negative as possible.

"Aye, aye, captain!" Benjamin mused, saluting the other-worldly being. He had a job to do in order to keep his boss happy. He aware what would happen if he didn't do what he was tasked with doing.

"Don't be foolish!" Jason hissed at the idiot. He was annoyed with Benjamin. He shook his head at the lad.

Benjamin frowned, harshly gulping as his childish behavior left him. He couldn't get what he wanted, acting a fool this time. "Sorry, sir."

"Don't apologize." Jason hissed, gliding away to leave his puppet where he stood. He growled at the male, "Come find me when you've gathered the three untamed, fire curses."

Further Revelations

Giovanni had been searching for Izzy who was usually ready for the day. He went to the younger boy's bedroom. He rubbed his eyes when he found Izzy cuddled into Fiona, causing him to furrow his eyebrows together. He had known Izzy to have some connection with the brunette girl, but he didn't think they held a non-platonic connection. He must have been wrong as he let a yawn escape his lips.

He ran a hand through his jet black curls as his silvery gray eyes finally came to their senses. He had dropped his habit of smoking cigarettes upon meeting the two lovely females at his school. He knew they wouldn't want to be around someone who smoked, "Hey, Izz?"

Izzy barely moved, forming a gentle smile on his lips. He was quite happy, and secure where he was. He tried to bury his face deeper into Fiona's abdomen. He forgot who he was with and where they gone.

Fiona grumbled in her sleep, disliking the movement. It took her a few seconds to recall the events prior, taking away the slither of panic she felt upon waking up in the home of someone she almost thought was a stranger. Her eyes fluttered as she began to stir causing her to rub at them.

Giovanni folded his arms to his chest while quite enjoying the innocent scene. He could tell Izzy might be attached to the older girl, but he was fairly certain nothing else would transpire. He already knew both of them so well even when he didn't know Fiona as long as he had known Izzy. He could tell the pair cared for each other— probably even loved one another, but even he knew romantic relationships took time. He was dressed in a black tee shirt with gray baggy pants, and red combat boots.

He was always up early—even on the weekends. He appeared in the doorway of Izzy's bedroom, because, didn't they have plans? The thought of loud knocking on the door was kicking around in his head until someone had to interrupt his thoughts. He parted his lips, casting his eyes over his shoulder.

"Boo!" Caleb said, gripping Giovanni from behind. He cracked a smile when the nineteen year old tensed in his spot. He was in a white tank top with khaki pants, and sandals. He was dressed like he would be going down to the beach.

Giovanni shot Caleb a scowl over his shoulder, "What are you doing?"

Caleb sighed, removing his hands from the shoulders of Giovanni. His fiery red locks were all over the place. He usually added some gel, but this time was different. "A brother can't tease another brother?"

Giovanni relaxed, "I wanted to wake, Izz. We have a meeting in the form of a study group today."

"Ah, so, little Isaiah has a girlfriend, already?" Caleb caught sight of Izzy cuddled into Fiona. He never saw the brunette becoming entangled with someone.

Giovanni shrugged, "They know each other from before Izzy became an orphan."

Caleb seemed to be lost in thought, mulling something over. He nudged Giovanni a little bit to get past him, "I have an idea on how to wake him!"

"I don't think your plan is going to go over so well with him." Giovanni said, fearful of what Izzy would do to Caleb. He was aware of the bitter dislike the younger boy had for the older boy, but why? He was beginning to believe that Izzy just didn't want an older brother in the form of the redhead, unsure of how to voice his thoughts. He did know that Izzy didn't mind hanging around him which was something else in it's own puzzlement.

Caleb pressed a finger to his pale pink lips as he snuck over to the younger boy. He was oddly enough, reminded of a baby mouse. He went to poke the younger boy in the back which was a big mistake on his part.

Izzy grew alarmed, grunting at the pain in his backside. His body was quite sensitive which is why he didn't like people touching him. He didn't hesitate to wake up, turning about to snap the pointer finger of Caleb, causing it to crack. "What the fuck is your problem? I don't like being touched!"

Caleb had tears, welling in the back of his eyes for the broken finger Izzy gifted him with. He shook his head as his vision blurred. "I, uh—"

Fiona's eyes shot open from all the commotion. She sat up, sitting crisscross. A look of guilt danced across her features. "I'm sure he meant you no harm, Isaiah."

"He was just waking you up for the study group date we had." Giovanni easily lied to cover for Caleb. He scurried over, shaking his head as he took a hold of the ginger boy.

Izzy scowled, feeling a tinge of guilt creep into his heart. "I warned, Caleb, before that I did bite."

"So?" Giovanni was evidently angry as he looked over the broken finger of the ginger boy. He internally groaned, tutting at the misery Izzy could easily caused. He cared for the boy like his actual brother yet Izzy was being ridiculous in his eyes.

Fiona bolted from the bed, exiting the bedroom. She came back a few minutes later with the first aid kit. "I know how to pop it back into place."

Caleb was in too much pain to respond. He was seething, clenching his teeth. All he could manage was a shaky, barley visible nod.

Giovanni cut his silvery gray eyes to Izzy, motioning for the eighteen year old to follow him from the bedroom. He was going to have a word with his newly cemented brother. Maybe, he could convince Izzy to quit hating Caleb.

Better Days

"Did you have to break his finger?" Giovanni inquired, gaining an eye roll from Izzy. He didn't believe the injury from Izzy was anything for the eighteen year old to be nonchalantly rolling his eyes at.

"I suppose not. It was an accident." Izzy said, sighing since he knew Giovanni was right. He didn't enjoy the disappointment flashing in the silver gray eyes of Giovanni.

"Well, you need to get dressed for the day." Giovanni spoke, becoming perky when his mind jumped to Sonya. He couldn't wait to see her—happy to have found the girl.

A hard yelp came from Caleb as Fiona fixed his pointer finger. The yelp from Caleb resonated throughout the entire house causing a scowl on the milky complected lad to become evident.

The two boys waited outside of Izzy's bedroom. They heard Caleb yelping as loud as day—if not louder. The older boy shot the younger boy a sharp glare.

Soon after the yelp, Fiona came out of the bedroom clutching her orange flannel jacket. She stopped next to Izzy whose dark mood lifted. "I'll see you pair later. I have to get home to change."

Giovanni nodded, "Sure thing." His jaw was clenched, still annoyed with Izzy for breaking Caleb's finger. He took deep breaths, trying to keep calm. He didn't want green flames to erupt from his palms once more.

Izzy bit his tongue to keep from pleading with Fiona to stay. He wasn't some clingy five year old boy. He shook his head, smiling at the brunette. "Don't get lost."

Fiona nodded before taking the stairs two at a time. She was out of sight, but not far from Izzy's mind. She would be relieved to change into a fresh pair of clothing, shuddering as she went.

Caleb proceeded to exit Izzy's bedroom. He stopped to clear the air. "Isaiah, I apologize for touching you. I shouldn't have done so. Don't hate me, alright?"

Izzy knew the least he could do was forgive the ginger for something he shouldn't have gotten all riled up about. It was him as a person nor could he help it. "I forgive you, Caleb."

Caleb could tell it was difficult for Izzy to say those four words. He was proud, beaming at how happy he was. "So, where are you two meeting your 'friends' for this study date?"

"The beach. I thought you already knew." Giovanni softly mused, grinning over at his brother. His eyes flickered from top to bottom of Caleb who was sporting a beach getup appearance.

Caleb shook his head, "How about you change it to the ice skating rink?"

Giovanni quirked an eyebrow up at the ginger. "Is Blossom interested in someone?"

Caleb shrugged. "I might like this beautiful girl I met in Spanish class."

"You don't take Spanish class." Izzy stated, folding his arms to his chest. His deep blue eyes were set on Caleb in curiosity. He didn't think the ginger was one to take the wrong classes either. He lifted an eyebrow, amused by Caleb's revelation of liking a girl.

"Yes, Buttercup, I know this." Caleb sarcastically remarked, giving a shake of his head. He could sense Izzy was starting to warm up to him after the incident.

"Melanie Stefani takes Spanish class. They say, she comes from an Italian-Mexican background." Giovanni perks up, shooting Caleb a teasing grin.

"Okay, so? You think I like her?" Caleb asked, unamused by his middle brother. He did his best to remain stoic on the topic.

Giovanni's grin nearly fell from his face. "If you don't like her in that way then why did you stick up for her?"

"I'm allowed to stick up for an innocent person without their being any other feelings attached, am I not?" Caleb rushed on ahead, growing angry at how everything had to be romantic.

Giovanni didn't like the way Caleb was behaving. "You know what, forget you, Blossom. Most guys don't help out those beneath them unless they like that person in a more than platonic way."

Caleb full on scowled at Giovanni. "The only girl I have ever liked is Sonya. You stole her from me."

Giovanni was baffled. He knew Sonya showcased no interest in Caleb. He spent enough time with the beautiful nineteen year old to know she wasn't a match for someone as erratic as Caleb. "A female isn't somebody who can be stolen from you, Caleb. She likes me and I like her. Move on, already!"

Caleb gifted Giovanni with a look of hatred. Sure, he might have held a connection with Melanie, but he had high hopes he could pass her off to Giovanni. He didn't think his orphan of a brother would steal the one girl he would die for, "Have it your way, Orphan Boy, but karma comes back around!"

Giovanni silently gasped. He didn't like to be reminded of his past. He had gotten along well with Caleb up until that point which made no sense to him. "You don't have to be so mean, Caleb! I thought we were brothers!"

A nasty look took hold of Caleb's fair features. "So did I, but I generally don't want to share my girl with you. Find someone else!"

Izzy gulped at the possibilities of what could transpire. He found his voice, clearing his throat to get the words out in order to intervene. "Guys, can we not fight? A girl is just a girl, no?"

"It's not like anyone is trying to steal Fiona from you, Isaiah. I mean, otherwise, why would you care about this argument?" Caleb rattled off to the eighteen year old who wasn't amused by the ginger.

Izzy shook his head in disagreement. "Fiona knows what she wants."

"I'm sure she does." Caleb said as an evil idea sprung to life in the back of his mind. He cracked his knuckles.

"Caleb, drop the subject. You're jealous she doesn't like you anymore. Get over it." Izzy spoke what Giovanni had been thinking. He was done with the arguing. He thought he had a breakthrough with Caleb like Giovanni had earlier on.

Caleb smirked, nodding. "You have a point, Izzy. Gio, I will move on."

Giovanni exchanged a look with Izzy as they watched him slink off. His worry heightened, knowing how Caleb hardly called them by their given nicknames—derived from their full names.

Not to Worry

Giovanni rolled his eyes. He had been waiting ages for Izzy to get dressed to meet the girls at the beach. He began to bounce his leg up and down as he called to the younger lad. "Hurry up, Izz!"

The bedroom door to the younger lad's bedroom opened. Out popped, Izzy with worry etched onto his features. "Is it possible Fiona doesn't like me the way that I like her?"

Giovanni frowned, "Don't let what Caleb said get to you. I'm sure she has some type of feeling for you."

"Yeah, for Oliver still." Izzy grumbled, tugging the black knit sweater of Fiona's over his dark blue long sleeve shirt. He wore regular blue jeans with dark sneakers. His eyes held concern in them along with a newfound bitterness.

"Unless the dead remain as spirits, how can you think like that? Did you ask if she still loved him?" Giovanni asked, pushing himself from leaning on the doorway. He began a seemingly slow trek down the stairs with Izzy.

"She said she never did, but who knows? She might be saying

things just to make me feel better." Izzy said, shrugging as his ever present pout returned.

"Do you feel like she was being genuine?" Giovanni suddenly asked as they left the house. He took out his car keys to his sleek, black car in order to unlock it. He was old enough to have his driver's license which Nazz Hemingway helped him to maintain.

"I do. Every word she said was true." Izzy spoke up, inhaling deeply. His shoulders grew relaxed.

"Then, force out the doubt. The doubt can create problems where there aren't any. Caleb being malicious all of a sudden doesn't help matters." Giovanni explained, starting up the engine once Izzy slid into the passenger side. He began the long drive as soon as they were both buckled up.

"Gio, you're a good, big brother. Oliver once had his good days, but when he found out about my shared kisses with Fiona then he changed." Izzy whispered, picking at his jeans for no apparent reason. He revealed more than what anyone had known.

Giovanni hadn't known Izzy was the riff between Fiona and Oso. He only knew there was a reasoning the pair lost contact. "Why would you hit on your brother's girlfriend? Who does that?"

Izzy sighed, becoming sad. "I didn't mean for it to happen. I was curious, and she was always so kind to me when no one else was."

"How long have you been into her?" Giovanni asked as a sense of foreboding caused the hairs on his body to raise. He could sense something was off, but not about the past of Izzy. He would be more alert if Izzy had been eleven, trying to hit on an older female. He knew by the time one hit teenage years they knew more of what they wanted; depending on the person—especially when one became eighteen.

"I can't say. All I can say is I made a move at the start of the year. The kisses kept happening until Fiona stopped it altogether. She thought it was wrong, but I didn't. However, I didn't try to press her anymore." Izzy spoke, upturning his palms in a shrug.

"How can you tell me, you don't know how long you've liked Fiona?" Giovanni asked, chuckling as he came to a stop at a red light. He made a mental note of how dim, dreary, and foggy the morning was.

"They started dating at my age. I did have a crush on her then, but I thought I'd grow out of it by the time I sprouted up. I tried to date this one girl my age, but it didn't last because apparently, I had no appeal to her." Izzy rattled off, feeling relieved upon getting the truth off of his chest.

"Was Fiona not your first kiss?" Giovanni grew confused. He didn't know his brother was close to being a player. His eyebrows were linked together.

"No, she was. I dated the girl after Fiona avoided me. I completely understood though." Izzy revealed as his eyes trailed up to the windshield. He finally took notice of how odd seeming the brink of day appeared to be.

Giovanni was frowning as the light remained on red for the longest time. His eyebrows met his hairline as he tapped his fingers on the steering wheel. "Why is it taking ages for the darned thing to turn?"

Izzy went to answer until his eyes landed on a black hooded figure. He paled, tensing as he noted how inhumane the creature like figure appeared. His heart began to pound in his chest whereas Giovanni saw what he was seeing. "I don't know, but what the fuck is that thing?"

"It doesn't even look human." Giovanni noted, shivering at the ominous feeling plaguing his body. His lips became parted upon cutting silvery gray eyes to Izzy.

Izzy slowly began to nod. "It looks like a Lord of Chaos. It's mentioned in the brown leather book Fiona left for me."

Giovanni slowly turned his head to fully look at Izzy. "She left you the book?"

"Yep." Izzy confirmed, nodding his head in confirmation. His eyes were laser focused on the figure gliding across their view. He didn't like what it possibly meant for their world.

Giovanni sat back as the creature glided away from sight. He shivered in fear, shaking it off as the light finally turned green. He proceeded to drive to the agreed destination. His mind still lingered on the Lord of Chaos.

Revenge

A smirk hung on the fair features of Caleb Hemingway. He didn't know why he was acting the way he was. He couldn't help the negative feelings washing over him. He didn't like what was becoming of him. He was wondering if it dealt with the fact that he had black flames.

He had been meant to meet up with Melanie at the ice skating rink, but he changed his mind. He pretty much ghosted the girl he liked. He opted to head down to the beach to hit up Fiona. He was planning to make Izzy pay for acting better than everyone else. He arrived where the group of four had a bonfire going in the midst of some trees.

He leaned on a tree, watching them enjoying the company of one another. He took a moment to realize just how pathetic they were. He was about to speak up when a cold chill of a shiver ran down his spine. The ominous feeling had been shifting his mood for quite awhile. He knew whatever was happening was somehow attached to him, because in his usual state—he wouldn't bother the four he was currently stalking.

Caleb took a deep breath. He moved forward, wandering into their view as he made his way over to them. He shot a smirk over to the boys. "Hey everybody!"

Izzy jumped in fright, but Fiona squeezed his hand for comfort. He allowed the action to calm his nerves, relaxing with her. He had this inkling that Caleb wasn't quite himself—for how long had Caleb been different?

Giovanni sighed, feeling his nostrils begin to flare up. "Blossom—"

"That would be Caleb to you, Sweetheart." Caleb corrected, Giovanni his sentence. His eyes drank in Fiona as a nasty smirk settled onto his milky features. He could take what he wanted with no consequences.

Giovanni groaned, "Take a seat, Caleb. Your mood swings are getting on my nerves."

Caleb grew sour, but took a seat on a log. He rubbed his hands together, "What did I miss?"

"Izz and I spotted a Lord of Chaos. It can influence those who maintain the fire magic curse." Giovanni said, briefly glancing to an ill seeming Izzy. He began to stroke his chin, trying to keep an eye on the redhead—just the same.

"Actually, fire magic is a gift—not a curse. The magic history books are almost always wrong." Fiona corrected the nineteen year old, simply shrugging her shoulders. She thought the information was worth knowing.

"Either way, seeing this Lord cannot be good." Giovanni spoke causing recognition to flash in Caleb's eyes. He felt a hint of relief clutch his heart, knowing Caleb was still buried within the depths of himself.

Caleb had heard the term Lord of Chaos before. He dug deep into his mind to voice what had been fucking with him. "I think that's why my behavior has been on again-off again."

"It would fuck with you, greatly. You hold the black flames which are harder to tame. You're strong." Izzy said, shooting the ginger a half smile. He was doing what he could to reassure Caleb.

Caleb wanted to smile at Izzy in return, finding the notion a difficult task. All he could manage was to further frown which was unlike him. How could his good mood sour upon living under the same roof as Izzy and Gio? He liked them as well as the band members of Linkin Park liked one another. It really didn't add up in his brain as he tried to drum up good thoughts alone, thinking that may save him.

"So, are my black flames meant to be evil?" Caleb softly asked in hopes to keep himself from his own negative mindset. His bad thoughts would turn him dark in a heartbeat. It wasn't something he was guessing, but something he deeply sensed.

"Eh, not necessarily." Sonya voiced, shaking her head. She felt guilty for rejecting the redhead—he didn't tickle her fancy. Nor could she stand lying to either one of them.

Caleb let his eyes travel to hers, causing a bit of anger to unravel in the pit of his stomach. He shook his head to fend off disruptive, dark thoughts. "Oh. Why would I be more susceptible then?"

"As Izzy already said, you're strong. The stronger you are, the easier it is for you to be susceptible." Fiona softly cooed as Izzy handed her the brown leather book. She began to flip through the pages which helped to distract Caleb.

Caleb had known his dark thoughts weren't his own. He sighed, gesturing to the book. "Will that help to clear the cobwebs of darkness attempting to run rampant in my head?"

Fiona shook her head, "Only you can fend off the darkness

nor does this darkness necessarily have to do with you."

"Fiona is right. It has more to do with the Lord of Chaos. The Lord of Chaos is what one would classify as the devil or as close as one can get to said devil." Izzy concluded as his eyes remained glued to the emerald green eyes of Fiona.

Fiona gently tapped her fingers on the book laying in her lap. She could see that the struggle in Caleb was real. She felt bad for him, wondering what could help him until the thought crossed her mind.

"Weren't you supposed to go ice skating with Melanie?" Giovanni suddenly asked, recalling the forgotten curvy girl. He didn't see why Caleb would skip out on Melanie.

Caleb gave a slight nod. "Sure, I was. I changed my mind at the last minute. Is that so wrong?"

"Wait, you ditched her?" Sonya asked, becoming outraged at the very thought. She wasn't inside the mind of Caleb nor did she know the inner turmoil he was dealing with.

"I didn't leave her in a ditch, if that's what you're asking." Caleb said, rolling his eyes at the brown complected girl. He wished he could have her even though she didn't want him. What was a guy to do? His eyes then traveled to Fiona intertwined with Izzy.

Trainwreck

"Fiona, could I talk to you in private?" Caleb mused with a slight twinkle of mischief in his eyes. He was about to put his plan into motion, unable to stop the evil growing in his mind.

Izzy nor Giovanni failed to take notice of their brother planning something. They managed to share a look—unsure of what to do. They we're wondering if they should speak up or let Caleb make his move; just to see what the redhead would do.

Fiona would have declined, but didn't feel like being rude. She was in a chipper mood ever since reconnecting with Izzy. She would do almost anything to make the boy happy. "Uh, sure?"

Izzy shook his head at Fiona, scowling as if to warn her against speaking with Caleb alone. "Don't!"

Fiona chuckled, ruffling his curls. "I'll be fine, Butterfly."

Izzy's heart nearly stopped in his chest. He did have a nickname, but he hadn't heard that one yet. He reached for her arm. "You don't understand—"

"I do." Fiona interrupted, lightly tapping his nose. She gulped, semi nervous to follow the lion into it's den.

Izzy was horrified by the possible outcome of what was about to happen. His deep blue eyes shot to Giovanni in alarm. He began to profusely sweat as his heart beat furiously in his chest.

Giovanni knew there was nothing he could say or do. He shot Izzy an apologetic look, "I don't know what you expect me to do. I'm sure nothing will transpire."

Izzy shot up from his seat on the log at the bonfire. His brother might be willing to sit idly by, but he wasn't about to. He would put himself in between Caleb and Fiona if the need arose. He wasn't worried about Fiona flirting or taking an interest in Caleb—he was worried about the redhead and his actions.

Caleb led Fiona towards an isolated path. He was glad to get the brunette alone. He was hoping she would lean up against a tree so he could make a move. His idea of revenge did involve hitting on the girl whether Isaiah liked it or not. "What do you see in that loser known as Isaiah?"

Fiona tensed, disliking the way the ginger spoke about his brother. "I fixed your finger, Red, so be careful how you speak of Isaiah. I can easily snap it again."

Caleb stalked closer like she was the prey whilst he was the predator. He was the reason her back met the bark of a tree. A half smirk sat on his features since he wasn't completely satisfied with getting her by her lonesome. "Fin—"

"That would be Fiona to you and everyone in the universe!" Fiona chillingly addressed Caleb, having became disgusted by the sudden gift of a new, less feminine nickname.

Caleb thought just maybe, her cold behavior was due to an attraction she didn't want for him. He pressed one of his hands to the tree just above her head. He dawned a smug smile, "What? Is Fiona unhappy with me or does she harvest a secret crush on me?"

Fiona rolled her eyes, huffing at his insinuation. "Sorry, Red, but I'm just not interested in you. You sorely lack adventure, and I pity the girl who actually likes you. I don't."

The smirk on his face was swiped off. His warm brown eyes turned to a hard glare. He pushed himself from the tree, beginning to pace in a circle in front of her instead. "I'm not the boring one, Fiona. You are."

"You know who you remind me of?" Fiona suddenly asked, moving from the tree—the trunk had begun to hurt her spine. She began to zip the zipper to her orange flannel jacket up. If looks could kill then she would be the winner in the department of 'killer looks.'

Caleb shrugged. "Shoot, girl, shoot! Your words won't harm me."

Fiona had recognized his behavior immediately. She noticed the way he spoke was a reminder of the one person she hadn't seen in ages. Her older brother had taken off when he turned eighteen nor did she know where he wound up. "You remind me of this boy I once knew, but much like Peter Pan he never grew up. He doesn't take responsibility for his actions like he should either."

Caleb froze in his tracks. He forced the negativity out of his heart and brain. He couldn't deal with how it was destroying his life. He shook his head to clear his thoughts. His eyes went from hard to their usual, caring warmth. "I don't like what's happening to me, Fiona."

Fiona could see the change in him. She also knew he wasn't lying. She nodded. "It's not you, Caleb. Somehow, you're attached to the Lord of Chaos via another person."

Caleb snapped his fingers, "I've heard that term before. I can't seem to place how I know Lord of Chaos."

"I know of one person who spoke in whispers about a Lord of Chaos." Fiona confessed to the redhead gaining a nod from him. Her mind almost went down memory lane, scowling as she tried to forget her older brother. Could he be behind what was happening in Orlando?

A crunch of leaves caught their attention. They shared a look, casting their eyes in the direction of the leaves crunching. Both of their eyes grew wide with fear—the possibility of the Lord of Chaos appearing was very real.

Izzy came into their view from around one of the dying oak trees, feeling relief flood his veins at how Caleb and Fiona had a distance between them. He had been walking at a slow pace to listen to their conversation. He was happy to overhear how Fiona wouldn't give in so easily. His heart soared with the knowledge.

"How are you able to keep the negative emotions out of your head then if you knew someone who spoke about a Lord of Chaos?" Caleb inquired causing Izzy to further relax.

Izzy walked over to Fiona, finding comfort in being near her. He craved her hand intertwined with hers, allowing patience to sink in. His eyes cut from Fiona to Caleb as he processed the conversation.

Fiona gulped, not entirely sure she knew herself. She could only play the guessing game. "I tend to embrace the negative emotions. I think that sort of helps—I also don't have fire magic."

Caleb nodded, wishing he could do the same. He was aware that brunette girl was right—unlike him, Fiona didn't hold fire magic in her veins. He did which would prove more difficult for him to fend off the darkness trying to override him.

Unfolding Honesty

Caleb, Fiona, and Izzy returned to the bonfire. He didn't bother to pry more information from Fiona about the person she knew, connected to the Lord of Chaos. He could tell she yearned to reiterate the story to the others. He just didn't know how the humane girl could embrace negative emotions without going insane. He would ask her more about the subject later, believing her to be hiding something from them.

It suddenly clicked in the back of his mind who would always mention the Lord of Chaos. His eyes widened as soon as realization dawned on him. "Benjamin went to my prep school."

Fiona furrowed her eyebrows, shaking her head at him. "Impossible."

"Why is it impossible?" Giovanni curiously asked her. He was doing what he could to gage reactions in order to see if they matched.

Sonya and Izzy also wondered how Fiona could possibly know it was impossible. Did she keep tabs on her older brother twenty four seven? What other information was she withholding from them?

Fiona gulped, clearing her throat. "Benjamin has never been rich. You have to have money to get into a prep school such as Bluejay Prep."

Izzy grew annoyed, having not been made aware of who Benjamin was to her. "Is he an ex-boyfriend of yours?"

Fiona shot Izzy a look of disgust. "Don't be gross, Isaiah. No."

"Who is he to you then?" Caleb curiously asked, yearning to pry the information from the brunette girl. He watched her shoulders drop in defeat—she couldn't keep secrets from them anymore.

"You recall the older brother I told you about?" Fiona inquired, wishing not to speak of her relatives. She despised her home life, but she was working on moving in with Sonya. She did what she could not mention her vile older brother by name—it was almost as if speaking the devil into existence before their very eyes.

Sonya had gotten Fiona a job at the Soy Bean Latte Cafe she would one day own. She was looking at two bedroom apartments they could share. She wanted to help Fiona have a better home life, considering her grades were circling the drain. She knew the topic of the older brother wasn't an easy one for her best friend. Her light gray eyes met the hard glare of the striking emerald green eyes belonging to Fiona.

"Yeah." Caleb softly replied, hating where the truth was heading. He was on the brink of putting two and two together.

"Well, his full name is Benjamin Calvert. He's a twenty eight year old with the audacity to trick those around him. He's a been a devil worshipper from day one which didn't help the friction with our parents." Fiona shakily confessed, wanting to rid the memories from her head.

"He's been attending the prep school for a good year." Caleb revealed, growing distraught by the truth coming from the lips of Fiona. How could they allow a twenty eight year old to attend Bluejay Prep? He should have checked the set ages since they were different than any other place he had heard of.

"Yeah, probably to keep an eye on you so he could target you." Fiona confessed, shivering at how uncomfortable she felt at the mention. She hated how her older brother always got away with everything especially when she was younger.

"He's a monster." Caleb revealed causing Fiona to nod with a faraway look in her eyes. If ever he met Benjamin again—he would make the gross male pay the piper. He couldn't forgive Benjamin for the death of Rory; his former best friend.

"I know from past experiences. He's always gotten his way by doing what he does best." Fiona replied, feeling quite ashamed to be related to the man they spoke about.

Izzy gave the hand of Fiona a gentle squeeze to reassure his beloved that she wasn't alone. He wanted her to know she had people surrounding her that she could count on.

"He killed my best friend right in front of my eyes. I haven't forgiven him nor will I." Caleb spoke aloud, gritting his teeth. He balled his hands into fists only to unclench them.

"I haven't forgiven him either for killing my best friend. My best friend was my—our little brother. He was only ten years old when Benjamin sacrificed him. Gosh, I hate even saying his name!" Fiona angrily revealed with tears, threatening to spill from her eyes.

Caleb felt a sting of an ache in his heart. His sympathy went out to the girl who lost her best friend to her other, more vicious brother. "I'm so sorry, Fiona."

Fiona sniffled, dabbing at her eyes. She forced away the

sadness, shivering in order to downplay it. She shrugged with slumped shoulders. "What can one do aside from get revenge?"

"I don't think revenge is the best solution." Izzy mumbled into her hand where his lips grazed her. He was practically leaning into the brunette who found some comfort of a distraction in his touch.

"I wasn't implying to get revenge on my brother, but to stop him; he might have to die. He's after the fire magic gift to resurrect his Lord of Chaos. I'm sure his bestie has a name." Fiona said, smirking as she rolled her eyes at Izzy.

Izzy copied her action in rolling his eyes. "Murder is not an option. Should it even be considered on anyone's behalf?"

"I'm sure you would lash out at him if he came at you, Izz or those you loved." Giovanni perked up, having sat himself by Sonya. He had long abandoned sitting by his lonesome.

Caleb grew curious about the sudden change of heart concerning Giovanni until a light, melodic voice called—startling, annoying, and distracting him.

"Hola, people! What's up?" Melanie Stefani quipped, coming into view while Caleb wasn't sure how to feel about her.

Caleb felt his heart almost stop in his chest. He forgot once more about his so-called connection with Sonya. He honed in on Melanie who plopped down beside him.

Melanie wore a soft pink skirt, black fishnet leggings, pink boots with no heels, and a long sleeve hoodie cut off. A smile spread to her eyes as she joined them. "Gio texted me something about a change of plans. I don't mind as long as we're together, Caleb."

Caleb grew mystified, but smiled over at the mixed girl. He wouldn't find anyone else as charming as her. He might have liked Sonya in a past life, but he had Melanie in his current life.

He should thank Giovanni later when he could since he invited her to the bonfire.

Jason

The day had grown into a long winded evening. The sun began to sink even if one could barely see it. The group of six had been sitting around while chatting in a good natured way. Everything seemed like it was going to be alright until night crept up on them, bringing dread with it.

Izzy tensed, holding onto one of Fiona's hands. His blue eyes darted about as if sensing something. He wasn't ready to take chances with what they couldn't see. A scowl became plastered to his full, pink lips.

Fiona could sense the dread Izzy was sensing. A frown hung on her features as her green eyes landed on the woods. She spotted the creature like being before the others saw it. Her eyes widened at the sight as her voice came out in a bit of a croak. "Oh fuck!"

Izzy's gaze mirrored hers, widening as he saw what Fiona saw. His hand squeezed hers tighter as the Lord of a Chaos drew closer to the group. He yearned for the darned thing to go away.

Untamed

"The name is Jason!" The Lord of Chaos growled out at them, startling those unsuspecting as it drifted closer to them. It wanted to be known, taking pleasure in the fright it caused.

Sonya gripped Giovanni who tensed upon eyeing the ugly creature. Her lips settled into a scowl, watching when Caleb opted to take a stand.

Caleb jumped up from his spot nearly tripping over Melanie in the process. He was tired of Jason and Benjamin. He was going to solve their problems—if it was the last thing he ever did.

Melanie didn't seem too phased by the fowl creature. She wasn't one who grew scared easily. She moved out of harm's way, wondering what was going to happen.

"Get away from us!" Giovanni growled as his free hand began to burn with green flames. He felt the energy surging to life in his veins, preparing to fight the vile creature of darkness.

Jason snarled in a bit of a chuckle at how ludicrous the boy was. He moved his head, shaking it in disagreement. "You cannot harm me!"

Giovanni ground his teeth together. "I beg to differ."

"Try it." Jason cooed in order to egg the nineteen year old into doing so, while chuckling at the dark haired boy. He knew if the three boys were bonded there was no way they could send him back from whence he came.

The cursed fire magic would strengthen him, because it was after all cursed. He wasn't anything good nor were they. Or so he had been lead to believe. Who didn't believe in the legend of the cursed fire magic?

Giovanni lashed out, blasting a ball of green fire at Jason which did burn him. He smirked to himself, but slightly frowned. He along with the others had been reading parts

116

from the brown leather book about the final bond. He still didn't know what it pertained to.

Izzy was on his feet with Fiona copying his action. He wasn't wondering if the Lord of Chaos would be obliterated by their colorful flames. He was tempted to stick out his hand, emanating in blue flames yet he refrained from doing so. He had been fearful of himself ever since the incident with his big brother.

Jason glanced from Giovanni to Caleb then to Izzy. He couldn't believe what he was bearing witness to. If he wasn't angered before then he definitely was rattled as they spoke. He found his current situation quite impossible, internally cursing Benjamin.

"Why does he look miffed like we won a bet?" Caleb asked, furrowing his eyebrows. He folded his arms to his chest, having been inquiring from his brothers.

Giovanni shrugged, unsure of how to respond. In truth, he didn't have the answers which wasn't a first.

Izzy watched in silence as fear struck the being hard. He began to softly stroke his chin. How could a Lord of Chaos become scared? Didn't they have no emotions, making them invulnerable? He refrained from sighing out loud as he mulled over the presence of Jason.

"H-Have you not bonded?" Jason inquired, meaning that the bond he knew hadn't been activated. He just wanted confirmation before he took off like a sissy. He was hoping that Benjamin was somewhere around to finish his dirty work.

A smirk flickered to life across Caleb's features. "What bond are you talking about?"

Of course, the three boys knew they were meant to bond. They just hadn't been sure of which bond. The book they had didn't necessarily come with clear instructions. They were slightly amused as Jason further shrinked on his spot.

Fiona remained silent, hating how someone she was raised with was a part of the current madness. She had known it had been a long time coming, knowing there wasn't much she could do. All she did know for sure is the future of Benjamin was about to be forever changed.

Jason didn't know if it would do the three boys any good to know or not to know. He needed them bonded, otherwise, how else was he supposed to maintain a mortal life? As expected a low moan of failure came from whatever Lord of Chaos he was. There was no good way telling of what he was—he just was. "It's the sibling bond!"

The stress in the Lord of Chaos' tone made it quite clear that he didn't come to play. He was more than certain of finishing what he started. His eyeless sockets slithered over Izzy, Caleb, and Giovanni—no longer amused.

Caleb, Giovanni, and Izzy all looked at one another in silent conversation. The boys had come across the sibling bond in the book with their girls. They seemed to speak with their eyes to one another, considering they didn't need the Lord of Chaos knowing what they were capable of.

"We haven't bonded." Caleb eagerly spoke, fully aware of the truth. He nonchalantly shrugged, acting as if the news didn't bother him.

Terror struck Jason who turned to glide away, farther into the woods. He wasn't sure where Benjamin was, but all he could do was hope he wasn't far which disgusted him. He was out of sight while the boys shared a look.

"Someone has to follow him, but somebody also has to wait for Benjamin. It's obvious, isn't it?" Giovanni stated, garnering confusion from Caleb who slowly grasped what the other slightly younger lad was saying.

"I'll go with you." Sonya volunteered, tightening her grip on Giovanni. She already knew he wanted to go after Jason. She was about to head off with her man when Fiona chimed in.

"I'll wait for my brother." Fiona bitterly spoke up, hating how she would see him again. Her skin crawled at the very reminder causing nausea and disgust to grip her.

Izzy nudged Fiona to remind her she wasn't alone. He would be staying with her which brought some comfort to Fiona. He saw the look on her face, further upsetting him. He had one thing in common with Fiona for sure—bad, older brothers.

"And, I'll go with Gio since it might be helpful to have two fire magical beings to rid the world of Jason. We might not be bonded, but we should dispose of him." Caleb said as Melanie agreed, opting to join the three—mostly on behalf of the redhead.

Benjamin

"What do you think is taking so long?" Izzy suddenly asked Fiona as a shiver ran down his spine. He began to grow anxious, waiting to see what was about to go down. He blew out a sigh in order to kick off the nerves.

Fiona smiled over at him, "I don't know. You sure are adorable though."

"Don't antagonize me." Izzy spoke, wringing out his hands. He was pacing back and forth around the bonfire. He wasn't expecting the older, distant brother of Fiona to actually show up.

Fiona chuckled, "I'm not trying to antagonize you, Isaiah. I'm sorry."

Izzy sighed, shaking his head of curls at her. "I don't mean to snap at you, but I'm a bundle of nerves as we speak."

Fiona frowned, nodding in understanding. "I truly didn't mean to throw you off balance. I'm just happy to have you back in my life. For a while I didn't think…"

Izzy heard the raw, genuine emotion in her voice stirring

120

something giddy in his heart. He reached out a hand instinctively to brush his fingertips across her jaw. He saw her visibly shiver in delight and comfort, causing his once cold heart to melt. "I didn't think I'd see you again either, Fiona. I wasn't sure I wanted to."

Fiona bit her bottom lip, "After what happened with Oliver. Yeah, I get it. I know he wasn't the best big brother to you, but I wouldn't wish death on my worst enemy."

Izzy felt a sting of guilt in his heart, but her eyes held a plea for him to not dwell on the past. He could tell she was just speaking the way she felt. All in all he did agree with her, "Why did you mention killing Benjamin if you're against death?"

"Unfortunately, it might be the only other option if—all doesn't pan out." Fiona spoke, not holding anything back from him. She upturned her palms, more nervous to see her older brother after all these years.

Izzy slowly began to nod as he stuck his hands gently into his pants pocket. "I don't wish death on my worst enemy. Like I said before, what happened to Oliver was an accident. I didn't know anything about the fire within."

Fiona stood up, nodding vigorously. She pressed her lips to his cheek, "Your parents were the ones responsible for telling you the truth. Never blame yourself for the unknown, Butterfly."

Izzy softly smiled at the brunette in his vision. His eyes almost wandered the rest of Fiona until a sense of dread washed over him. He stiffened in his spot. "Do you feel that?"

Fiona tensed, gripping Izzy's hand as she turned to eye their surroundings. She felt disoriented, putting her on high alert. She refused to let anything bad happen to Izzy, especially after everything he had gone through. "I definitely feel the negative, draining emotions meaning one thing."

"What?" Izzy asked, tilting his head causing some of his curls to graze her chin. He was eight inches taller than her, towering over her for a guy one year younger than her.

"He's here." Fiona said as she kept steadily glancing about the area. She was trying to gage which way Benjamin was going to appear.

Izzy could tell by her tone that Fiona was implying her brother was present. Who else could it be if not the one person who brought the Lord of Chaos to life? He didn't have anything else to say as it happened.

"My dear sister, you would be correct. I am here." The voice of Benjamin Calvert rang out. He appeared in the clearing of the woods as waves viciously crashed not far from the beach. A malicious smirk placated his features with dark eyes.

"He might as well as be into old men." Izzy mumbled in a low whisper to Fiona. He was being sarcastic while attempting to remain serious—given their current predicament. Of course, the sight of the older boy in a black kilt didn't help him think differently nor did he have a closed mind. He just hadn't been exposed to males in drag which was something he could live without.

Fiona knew all too well about guys like her brother. She folded her arms, blocking Izzy from view as she pushed him behind her. She wasn't about to put him in harm's way, not after she lost Oliver. She might not have been in love with her ex-boyfriend, but she still grieved him like any normal person would. "Izz, now is not time for the absurd, rude jokes!"

Izzy tinted pink at how she called him out. He didn't mind, knowing he would apologize later. He held respect for those who could maintain a healthy relationship even the oddball, weird natured couples of the universe. He grew quiet as Benjamin stood there, rubbing his hands together.

"Fiona, how have the abusive parents been?" Benjamin inquired, gaining a startled gasp from Izzy. He was revealing information to Izzy that he didn't know about Fiona.

Fiona might have tensed, but she knew she would eventually talk into the morning hours with Izzy about it. It's how they both fell asleep. Sometimes, they would fall asleep early into their talks, but their conversations would finish the next day during breakfast or lunch. Sometimes, the conversations would finish the following night. "You are not allowed to call me by name or even a nickname."

Benjamin grunted as he held up a hand. He took a shot at his sister, but Izzy maneuvered to where he was in front of Fiona. His darkened eyes widened, aware of what Jason would do to him—if he took out the curses especially before they sealed their bond.

The Final Bond

Izzy held up his hands which were engulfed by blue flames. He had moved in front of Fiona so she wouldn't die by the hands of her older brother. He was sure he could finish Benjamin off with no qualms about it. "You don't get to touch her!"

Benjamin growled, hating how his family reunion was suddenly interrupted. He glared at the boy in his view through nothing, but his black eyes. His yellow fingernails were out nor was he messing around. "I want my sister dead!"

Fiona felt a bit of a tear in her heart. She had always shared bad blood with him, but she didn't think he would want her dead. "Why would you want me dead?"

"I don't want to have to worry about my family anymore. Our parents are dead, and I saved my precious baby sister for last." Benjamin growled with a smirk splashed across his features.

Fiona couldn't believe her ears upon hearing what her brother said. She heard the confession in his tone; loud and clear. "You k-killed them?"

Benjamin grinned, rubbing his hands together. "I did. You're my final target, Fiona."

Fiona shouldn't be shocked. If their parents were dead then she would have to be next. Of course, she wasn't close with them, but that didn't mean she wanted them dead. "I still don't get why you would want me dead. I've done nothing wrong to you."

"I don't want to have to worry about familial ties. Why is that such a hard concept for you to grasp?" Benjamin reiterated in a growl. His smirk had dropped, because of how clueless his baby sister appeared.

Fiona finally understood in that moment that he never once cared about family. She understood he cared about no one unless it benefited him, further shattering her heart. She felt bad at the same time she knew what would unfold wasn't her own doing. She sighed, dropping her shoulders in defeat as Izzy shot her a quizzical look over his shoulder. She didn't bother to glance at the boy, considering what they both knew had to happen.

"At least, I didn't betray my best friend." Fiona spoke in a bit of a growl to Benjamin. Her brother was cold, heartless, wretched, vile—all the twisted names one could think of.

Benjamin simply chuckled in a bit of a low growl. He shrugged, uncaring about her words. He lifted one hand in order to dig his yellow fingernails at them when Izzy beat him to the punch. He was halfway to finishing his job assigned to him by Jason.

"Not today, Devil Worshipper!" Izzy vehemently shouted, blasting the older male with blue flames. He shielded his eyes once the flames engulfed Benjamin who let a piercing yelp rip from his lips. He felt guilt tug at him all the same as he tried to bury the emotion deep within as Benjamin screeched like the demon he was.

Fiona didn't even know she had tears, trailing down her cheeks until they began to dry on her face. She shouldn't be crying for a bad man, but she did wish she could have done more to save her brother. Ever since, she was a child she could see how far gone her big brother had been. She would try to be compassionate towards him while managing to try to be there for him. She would be shrugged off with no care in the world like she was a great nuisance to her big brother.

Izzy grimaced as Benjamin turned into a pile of ash. He knew the demonic boy had been cleansed of his evil ways. He just couldn't help, but to wonder if he went to Heaven or Hell if said places even existed. He turned to Fiona who was shaken up causing guilt to widen his eyes. "Fiona, I—"

"Don't apologize. It was him or us." Fiona quickly interrupted Izzy, beginning to wipe her tear stained cheeks. She tried not to let the downfall of Benjamin get under her skin.

Izzy turned to Fiona, using a thumb to wipe a stray tear from her face that she had missed. "Still, I am sorry. He was family which hurts either way that you view the outcome."

Fiona softly chuckled at the boy, nodding her head in agreement. She smiled as she pulled Izzy closer to her. "I know, and it does."

Izzy went to reply when the others returned, but they looked rather rough. He froze from further touching Fiona, raising an eyebrow at the group. His lips were parted, waiting for them to speak up.

Giovanni had torn jeans with a gash in his tee shirt. He looked worse for wear with blood on his lips. He felt good— overflowing with adrenaline. He could shoot more green flames and feel good about the events.

126

Melanie and Sonya seemed unscathed, but breathed heavy due to having to keep up with their respective guys. They were unsure if they even wanted to stick around. They kept shooting wary glances at one another.

Caleb had dirt on one side of his face with blood smeared on the other side. He looked rather displeased. "The Lord of Chaos was slain— thrown back where he dug himself up from. However, the actual devil probably has him bobbing for apples."

The words struck relief in Izzy and Fiona who smiled at each other due to the good news. They couldn't be more thrilled for the revelation.

Izzy stepped away from Fiona towards his brothers. "I truly am grateful to have you as my brothers. You might not be blood, but family is family—blood or optional."

Caleb and Giovanni exchanged a similar smile before stepping towards Izzy. They were about to pull Izzy into a hug when something occurred. It had been worth waiting for and they knew as much.

The three boys stuck their hands in a circle, making a pact which bound them. A black light, a green light, and a blue light erupted from each boy to engulf them. The three boys were officially bound as brothers who would die for one another. It also tasked them with protecting one another's girlfriend or respective partner whenever in a crisis. However, the boys knew their girls could take care of themselves; no matter, the danger they got into.

Their adventure had come to a close for the time being. Nor would any of them believe they would be prepared for the future. They smiled at one another, believing the good times would last.

About The Author

Madaline Clifton has been writing for years—ever since she was a child. She loves nature (minus what can kill her in nature) with a love for cats; owning two. She's a southern woman with scoliosis and anxiety. She writes, sometimes she reads, other times; she listens to music or binge-watches her favorite show; Charmed (1998). A person can indeed change their stars, given the right circumstances or chance.

Milton Keynes UK
Ingram Content Group UK Ltd.
UKHW020631140524
442690UK00001B/28